PEEP SHOW

PEEP SHOW

EROTIC TALES OF VOYEURS AND EXHIBITIONISTS

EDITED BY
RACHEL KRAMER BUSSEL

CLEIS
PRESS

Published in the United States by Cleis Press Inc., P.O. Box 14697, San Francisco, California 94114.

Printed in the United States.
Cover design: Scott Idleman
Cover photograph: Barnaby Hall/Getty Images
Text design: Frank Wiedemann
Cleis Press logo art: Juana Alicia
First Edition.
10 9 8 7 6 5 4 3 2 1

ISBN: 978-1-57344-370-8

Contents

INTRODUCTION: HUNGRY EYES AND SENSUAL SHOW-OFFS

When the stories started rolling in for *Peep Show,* I was surprised to see that so many were about sex work: strippers, burlesque babes, and other professional show-offs and their customers. I had intended the title to be a sexy suggestion of the complementary fetishes of exhibitionism and voyeurism, not necessarily the main setting for the bulk of the stories. As I kept reading, though, I realized that peep shows and other forms of commercialized sexual displays are a major way we as a culture sanction—and control—the act of watching.

There's a sense of the forbidden in many of the stories you'll read here, whether money changes hands or not. There is the thrill of baring your body in exactly the place you're not supposed to, which Lolita Lopez zeroes in on with her nude campus performance art protagonist in "Indecent." As Lopez writes, "Trini couldn't stop herself. The risk heightened the allure." In Malcolm Ross's "Sleeping Beauty," the main character catches his gorgeous wife in repose in the middle of the night, and is compelled to keep on watching. M. March gives us a poignant, moving story of being watched over from above.

As for those peep shows, there's plenty of very sexy jiggling to be seen here. Donna George Storey beautifully and, as always, utterly erotically captures a different kind of peep show in "Clean and Pretty," in which an American woman in Japan soaps up in the shower, getting paid handsomely, while exulting in the one viewer who can look for free. Geneva King takes us deep inside Amsterdam's famous red-light district, or *"Rosse Buurt."* A woman is drawn to a woman she sees there, a woman who "stands in her window on the second story, not banging on the glass like the other girls, just standing, surveying the crowd, like she picks the customer and not the other way around, like she's deciding who is lucky enough to experience any bit of her." This is the kind of woman who sells her body in this book; one who's knowing, aware, yet can allow herself to get swept away by passion, even when she's on the clock.

Modern technology also plays a role here in the webcam-themed "Audience Participation" and "I've Only Got Eyes for You," where private citizens become amateur porn stars. When you think of voyeurs, you probably picture the iconic image of the Peeping Tom, and he's to be found in these pages as well, once, even wearing a trench coat. But rather than being the town creep, here the various peeping Toms (and Thomasinas) are more than just stereotypes. They see and hear things they aren't supposed to, and sometimes, as with Sommer Marsden's Jared in "Satisfaction Guaranteed," they even get caught.

Neighbors, coworkers, spouses, and hotel guests all experience the power of looking, and being looked at. Even the most intimate relationships can get closer when one person opens himself up to being studied, caressed not with the hands but with the eyes. These stories honor the art of the striptease, the daring of the nudist, the boldness of the person who'll go out of her way to get more than an eyeful. I hope the sensual visions these stories create stay in your mind's eye for a long time to come.

Rachel Kramer Bussel
New York

SHOWTIME

Susan St. Aubin

Whenever Lesley talks about him, I have to restrain myself or I'll drool into my latte or ice-cream soda or whatever we've decided to go out for on our afternoon breaks. She's perverse, preferring ice cream in winter, saving hot drinks for summer. That's one of the things I like about her.

"Ellie, he wears these bike shorts," she says in a voice much tighter than I imagine his pants are. "You can see every bulge, like a dancer, except, well..." She moves her hands down as if she's sculpting his body. "More unrestrained. He doesn't wear a jockstrap, or underwear, just the tights. Short ones, down to about midthigh, with his muscles bulging over." Her tongue clicks with disapproval. "He waltzes out to his exercise bike, which is right in front of his picture window, which faces mine. If I have the lights on, he *knows* I can see him, but he ignores me. He gets on slowly, shifting himself like guys do so his things won't get caught between him and the seat, settles himself down and just pedals away, going nowhere. Sometimes he's facing me, coming right at me, other times his back is to me so I can see his buttcheeks going up and down. It's an invasion of my privacy, that's what it is."

She digs her spoon into her glass and scrapes out the last bit of ice cream, shoving it into her mouth.

I look down at the chocolate sauce pooled in the bottom of my glass, thinking how I wouldn't mind an invasion like that.

"You don't know how it makes me feel," she says. "He's like an intruder breaking into my house. Our windows are so close we might as well be in the same room."

"Have you tried looking away?"

"Our windows face each other over a small courtyard. He's so close I can practically hear him breathe. How could I not look?"

I do drool then, more than the treat warrants, and lick my lips, pretending it's just the chocolate sauce.

She's already described his slick, silky black shoulder-length hair, which he doesn't tie back but lets dangle over his face until it's damp with his sweat. She's told me how he pumps his powerful arms up and down on the bicycle handles to exercise them, and how his fingers move as he adjusts the tension on the bike while he's pedaling, his legs flexing and straining. Not to mention his bare, hairless, tanned and glistening chest, with firm muscles that push his nipples out almost like breasts.

"He must spend a lot of time at the gym," she says. "I'll bet he does nothing but work on his bod all day, and then he comes home and *pedals his way right into my space!*" As she says each word, she drums her spoon on the round, metal table where we sit in the ice-cream parlor around the corner from our office. A couple of other die-hard winter ice-cream eaters are turning their heads, glancing at her while trying not to look, but she has no shame. "I really resent him!" she almost shouts.

Here I should mention that although she's just turned sixty, Lesley is an attractive woman—nice figure, hair dyed a natural-looking shade of auburn (maybe it *is* natural, though at her age, you'd think she'd have some gray), and a face that, while not exactly fresh and young, is still pretty much unlined. When she smiles, she looks thirty-five, easy. She dresses well, usually in pants or straight skirts, not too snug, not too loose, and sweaters cut just low enough to reveal the barest hint of cleavage.

She's my mother's age, but not at all like a mother, perhaps because she never had kids. We get along; we go out to lunch and on breaks together and talk about everything. She's my friend, as well as my supervisor in the law office where I sit at a computer typing legal documents all day. If it weren't for her, I'd be bored out of my mind.

"I'd ask him over for dinner," I tell her.

She makes that clicking noise with her tongue. She's been widowed for three years, so we share dating stories like single women do. l know she dates lots of men and sometimes even sleeps with them, but in spite of her detailed descriptions, she claims this one isn't for her.

"He's just a shallow young guy," she says, putting down her spoon. "There's nothing there, you know, Ellie?" She points to her forehead.

"How do you know? Why not give him a chance?"

She clicks her tongue again.

Maybe that's the age difference speaking. I'm twenty-four and can enjoy a shallow young dude now and then, in his place, while Lesley says she's more excited by fine wine and good conversation. For her, the whole point of a date would be the gourmet meal she'd cook for him, or the play or film they'd see together. Sex might be no more than a nice afterthought to a great evening, rather than the main course. She seems more concerned about what they'd have to say to each other than what they could do with each other.

On some of my best dates, we just go straight to bed and forget about dinner and the movie. We drink wine after. I can imagine Lesley's neighbor knocking on my door; I can see myself leading him straight to the bedroom while the game hens burn. We'll order takeout from the Hickory Pit later. Much later.

"Were you *always* so particular?" I tease, guessing she was more like me when she was younger, and maybe still is, deep inside. That's why we like each other.

"Oh, nonsense!" she explodes. "You make me sound like some fussy old maid. I just don't want that man in my living room."

"Have you tried curtains? I could make you some, and help you hang them." I haven't been over to her place since this man came into her life, so I want to see for myself what he's like.

"Why should I be the one to put up curtains? Why should I have to block out my light and air and view—yes, I still have a bit of a view to the side of his building. I can see a sliver of the bay and the lights of the city. Drapes would cut off that part of the window even when they were open. Everyone else who's lived in that apartment kept their curtains closed. When we first moved in we had a gorgeous view of the city, before that building went up six years ago. We never needed curtains."

She's quiet then. I know she's thinking of her husband and his sudden death from a heart attack when he was just fifty-nine.

"Oh, come on, Lesley. I bet you can't wait to get back home and watch your own private porn flick," I say, to cheer her up.

She doesn't laugh. "Time to get back to work," she says in her best supervisor voice, and marches out of the ice-cream parlor, which is empty now.

* * *

I imagine Lesley arriving home at night. It's six o'clock when she puts her key in the door and pushes it open, and dark because it's January. She goes in but doesn't turn on the lights yet. The city sparkles at the edge of his window, which is a blank, dark space. She sits in one of the two revolving chairs, now turned toward her stereo and a wall of books instead of the window. She slowly revolves to the view.

Across the way, the lights come on. The young man, whose name she hasn't tried to discover, walks slowly in, wearing only his tight short pants, a towel around his neck. The pants are like black plastic molded to his body. He mounts his stationary bike, which faces her this time, pulling himself up with his muscular arms while sucking in his impossibly flat abdomen. He smiles because even though he can't see his audience in the dark, he knows she's there. Her apartment is the theater; his, the stage. He pedals carefully at first, then faster, more recklessly, as if he plans to crash through her window and land at her feet, her slave forever.

She's breathing faster, in time with his pedaling. Is that her hand unzipping her pants, slipping her fingers down? She raises her hips and rocks back and forth in her chair as he spins into her.

But that's just me. I'm sure Lesley always turns on her lights the minute she walks in, just like she does when I come home with her one night.

"You see how nice it is now?" she says, motioning out her window, where we can see the stars and city lights that surround the blank bulk of the building across the way. To one side is a sliver of the dark bay. Lesley's living room is reflected in his window so we can watch ourselves as we shed our coats.

"It was so great when my husband and I first moved in,

before that thing was there." She gestures dismissively at his building, and heads for her small but conveniently arranged kitchen, with exotic spices alphabetized in wooden racks, and copper pans hanging on the wall above the gleaming black gas range. The refrigerator opposite is built into the wall along with the cupboards.

"I've made fresh pesto," she says, "so we can have some with my pasta and some sausage."

Her pasta-making machine sits on the counter. From the kitchen, I can look out her living room window. I'm waiting for him.

"I can see why you don't want curtains," I murmur, and then quickly correct myself. "I mean, this is like being in a tree house." Actually, it's not because the fifteenth floor is too high up to see any trees. "You could get the kind of curtains that rise up above the window, like on a stage," I tell her. "Then the side view wouldn't be cut off. And any time you want to see him, you could just raise…"

"Oh, for goodness sake, I do *not* want to see him, that's the point. I guess it would be nice to be able to cut off his show when his lights go on."

"Sure," I encourage her. "Have it both ways—your view when he's not home, and, well, when he gets on his bike, you have a choice. Up or down."

She laughs. "Down," she says, firmly.

There's a sale on at Macy's, where they have exactly the kind of curtain she needs, so I go downtown with her one Saturday to have a look at it.

"Window dressing," the saleswoman calls these curtains.

"No more window undressing," Lesley murmurs.

As we giggle together, I'm imagining him undressed, riding his bike toward me while I stand at her window, pulling my sweater over my head, shaking my long hair loose, deftly unhooking my bra, then letting it drop. I want to crash through his window and land on his handlebars; I want to feel his naked, sweating shoulders as I sink my tongue deep into his mouth.

This kind of curtain is more complicated than anything I could possibly make, so Lesley orders it to be delivered and installed the next Saturday. I tell her I want to be there to see how it works.

Late Saturday afternoon, after we've been drinking wine while waiting for the delivery, two hunky men finally arrive, carrying big boxes. This is even more elaborate than I thought it would be. They nail a frame around the window and attach a pulley before they actually hang the curtain. It's automatic, with a remote control Lesley holds in one hand, studying it while they work.

When the installation is finished, one of the men, my favorite, who wears a tight red river-driver's shirt with the buttons undone, and heavy black work boots, smiles at me as he says to Lesley, "Okay, bring it down."

When Lesley points the remote, the curtain slowly unfurls.

I'm still high enough to wink at the man, but he gets suddenly shy, and looks back at the descending curtain. It's kind of like a blind made of glimmering silver cloth, and when it's down, the room seems to glow. I applaud.

Lesley isn't so sure. "Well, it's all right," she says. "And anything's better than nothing, you know."

The guys don't know, so they look at each other. I try to catch river-driver-shirt's eye, but he ignores me.

"Well, thanks," Lesley says, dismissing them. We all think she might offer a tip, but she doesn't, so they pack up and go.

"Losers," I mutter, angry at river-driver.

Lesley nods in agreement as she pours us another glass of wine. "They've got nothing to say to me."

I'm beginning to see what she means, but still, I shrug. "I don't care about talk," I say.

She ignores that. "I've got some leftover rabbit stew from my dinner party last night," she says. "Want to stay and have some?"

Bunny stew. What will these gourmets come up with next? My stomach turns a little, but I do want to see what happens with bicycle guy. And the stew is wonderful, the meat a lot like chicken, but richer, sweet and tender. She serves it with a dry, fruity sauvignon blanc. I'm learning the names of wines from her.

After dinner we sit in the two revolving armchairs in her living room, facing the silver curtain.

"I feel like a prisoner," she complains. "I should have gone with blue. That silver color reminds me of iron bars on windows."

"No it doesn't," I protest. "It's the color of the moon."

She stares at the curtain, shaking her head.

"Listen, I could show you how to watch, on your own terms." I want her to enjoy this opportunity as much as I would if I lived in her apartment. "The thing is, it's best if he doesn't know you're here. Do you think he's on his bike yet?"

"He's usually out Saturday nights."

"Good. Then turn out the lights and we can raise the curtain before he gets in. That way, we can see him but he can't see us."

"We might have a while to wait," she says. "If it's late he won't want to ride. And if he has a girl with him, they'll just go into the bedroom. Or he might not even come home until tomorrow."

I suck in my breath. So, she *does* watch him. I sense an opening, a hint of desire.

"All right, maybe tonight his girlfriend will throw him out," I say. "Maybe he'll come home all frustrated and take it out on his bike."

She gets up suddenly and turns out the lights. I pick up the remote and raise the curtain.

His apartment is a black hole opposite us. I strain my eyes but can't see a thing.

Lesley sits down next to me, and takes the remote. "Just in case he gets too gross," she jokes.

"What do you mean?" I'm wondering if he takes off those shorts, gets a hard-on, points it at her. What has she seen?

She shrugs. "All he does is ride, but you never know what might happen."

We wait. We move to the sofa beside the window. Lesley turns on the lights long enough to make and serve coffee, then turns them out again. Even on the fifteenth floor, there's a dim glow in Lesley's living room from the lights of the city. We pretend not to look out the window, until a flash of light makes us turn our heads.

He's there: alone, fully dressed in jeans and a black turtle-neck, wearing a long black coat, which he takes off and throws on his sofa. He raises his arms and stretches.

"Eleven-thirty is early for him," Lesley remarks. "He usually brings a girl home, but never the same one twice." She picks up a pillow and buries her face in it, as if she regrets revealing how much she actually does watch him. "Often he doesn't come home at all," she mutters into the pillow. Perhaps the darkness makes it easier for her to talk about him.

I'm disappointed when he leaves the room. "Does he ever change into his bike shorts in front of the window?" I whisper, as if he could hear me, but he's not even in the living room. I mean, his living room. His presence is so strong I know what Lesley means: he has invaded us.

She's huddled in the corner of the sofa now, clutching her pillow. "I've never seen him change his clothes," she says. "I don't know if I could watch." The curtain control dangles limply from her fingers.

"Oh, come on. He *wants* us to watch!" I move to one of the chairs for a more direct view, but she stays on the couch.

"You're enjoying this, aren't you?" she says, accusingly.

"Well, yes." I'm already starting to feel a little breathless.

"That's because you're young. I'm past all that ridiculous lust, falling for totally inappropriate men I'd never want to talk to or even see again."

So. She fell for him. I swivel around to face her. "You don't ever have to talk to him. That's the beauty of this setup," I explain. "And the curtain gives you the power to watch only if you want to. He's not a person you'll ever have to deal with. He's like..." I search for the right word. "A computer game, or a movie. He's not real. You have the power to turn him on or off."

When he walks into the room in his tights and gets on his bike, my heart flops over. I couldn't turn him off if I wanted to. He's real. "Showtime!" I say with a clap of my hands.

I swear he looks at us. Is it possible he sees us in the dark? He nods as if he senses we're there. He stretches his legs and flexes his arms. His muscles ripple. I can feel my pulse pound in my clit. I look over at Lesley. She's put the pillow down and turned her head toward the window.

He begins to pedal, slowly at first, then harder, faster. In the dark I unzip my jeans, slipping my hand in to find myself already wet enough to slide my fingers around. He pumps himself up and down on the handlebars until I see sweat begin to break

on his forehead and trickle down his face. He wipes it away
and shakes his head. His powerful arms gleam damply in the
light of the lamp beside his bicycle. His mouth is open. He must
have set the bike to UPHILL—his chest heaves and his leg muscles
contract. He reaches down to reset his speed and pedals slower,
stretching his arms out to his sides, then waving them in slow
circles to unkink the muscles.

I look over at Lesley, who is reclining on the couch, her slacks
unzipped and pulled halfway down her thighs. She doesn't think
I can see her in the dark, or maybe she's forgotten I'm there. I
have a sense of déjà vu, not because I think I've been here before,
but because I know she has, more than once. I pull my hand out
of my pants and just watch, turning my head back and forth
from the rider to the lady on the couch, which is how I'm beginning to think of them as I wonder where they'll go.

He's riding faster again, staring directly into Lesley's living
room, his eyes dark, his brow furrowed, keeping up a steady
pace. Her hand moves in time with his pedaling. The room is
silent except for her breathing, an intake of breath every time
he pushes down on a pedal. Up, down, up, down; in, out, in,
out. I'm hypnotized by his bare feet that clutch the pedals, by
her breaths, which come as intensely as those of someone on
life support, as if his pedaling is keeping her alive. We're all
suspended in the sky, fifteen stories up, held in place by fragile
frames of wood, concrete, steel, and belief, all of which might
collapse in seconds in an earthquake. I'm afraid I feel the building
begin to shake. I fix my eyes on what I can see of his crotch. Is he
erect? Will his come when she does? I can't tell.

"Oh!" she moans. "Ah."

He pedals, pedals, until she gives a high cry, like a bird
taking flight. He stops, then, kicking his legs out to the sides and
throwing his arms in the air. His hair fans out as he shakes his

head, sending droplets of sweat flying, glimmering golden in the lamplight around his forehead. He leans on the handlebars, his hair hanging down. And yet, he can't have seen us.

She's breathing slower now; it's my breath that comes quicker. I find my cunt wet and swollen as my hand creeps back into my jeans. I can feel my pulse throb there. But I think I ought to leave; I feel Lesley wants to be alone now since she still hasn't said a word. She lies with her slacks still down, and in the light from his living room, I can see moisture glistening in the hair between her legs.

He looks up, takes a deep breath, and climbs off his bike, wiping his head with a towel he picks up from the floor beside his exercise bike as he walks out of the room. I think I should ring down the curtain now, but I don't know where the remote is. Lesley had it last but I don't see it anywhere near her. My fingers twitch against my swollen clit. Should I come or should I go? His lights go off, though I didn't see him come back into the room. Probably there's a switch in the hall. I hope he's going to bed happy. I know I will. My hand moves faster but I'm as silent as a child who doesn't want her mother to find out what she's doing, although I'm sure Lesley wouldn't mind. This is her home and she's just had sex with her nameless neighbor and now she's breathing calmly, like someone who's fallen into a deep sleep, so she'll never know that when I come, the city lights seem to pop like fireworks beside his dark, blank windowpane.

After a minute I stand up, find my bag and jacket, and tiptoe to the door. Her steady breathing tells me she hasn't heard a thing. I let myself out.

She never speaks of him again, and I don't ask. When I visit her, the curtain is always down. Sometimes at work, though, I see her smile as she gazes at her computer screen like she's looking through a different window, where the curtain is rising.

CLEAN AND PRETTY

Donna George Storey

My intercom buzzes again for the fifth time tonight—or is it the sixth?

I wipe my oily hands on a towel, slip on my cotton robe and press down the button.

Hiro's husky voice slithers into my ear. "Jenny-san? You've got another customer. He's ordered 'Virgin's Forbidden Pleasure' and 'Breast Soap Show.' Oh, and he says he wants 'Total Satisfaction.' "

"Don't they all?" I turn toward the security camera and grin. I can't see Hiro, but I can imagine his lips stretching into a wry smile, like we're laughing at the world together.

His voice softens. "Are you tired? You are very busy tonight."

"That's because I'm so clean and pretty. Or at least that's what the expert tells me." I say this all in English and strike a vamp's pose.

He laughs, a low chuckle that twines itself around my chest and squeezes. Time stops, suspended in the hot, damp air. My belly contracts, a sharp sexual twinge. But this is business. As much as I try to forget this, Hiro never does.

"Your customer will be there in a few moments. Thank you again for your hard work," he adds in brisk Japanese. The intercom goes dead.

I'm alone again. But that's my job—to be a woman alone with her fantasies.

I lean into the shower stall and start the water. Steam rises up over the glass walls, which don't quite reach the ceiling. In no time, the small room will be thick with mist. It won't be too thick, however, to obscure the figure of a naked woman washing herself for any observer who may have slipped into the room. The careful placement of the spotlights guarantees the honorable customer gets what he's paid for.

I shrug off my robe and hang it on the hook embedded in the mirrored wall. The place really does look like some posh hotel in miniature. Hiro told me he pays special attention to detail for the design of each new club. Reality is the essential foundation of every fantasy, he said, and this was every man's dream, to spy on a girl making herself clean and pretty in a lavishly appointed bath. I'm not sure if it's true, but I do know bathing is an important ritual in Japan, a form of purification that dates back to ancient times. With separate facilities in most public baths in hot springs and inns, the thrill of peeping in on the ladies was no doubt a potent taboo. Hiro readily agreed with my theory, but when I asked if he personally had a thing about watching a girl masturbate in the shower, he only smiled.

The intercom buzzes a brief warning, and I move into action, stepping under the spraying water, my eyes half-closed. The door clicks open. I see a sliver of light from the hall widen then disappear with another click of the latch. Of course, I give no sign I know I'm being watched.

But I do know. It's time for the show to begin.

I arch my neck, letting the water stream over my face and hair. The pose alone suggests innocent wantonness. My lips part, my breasts tilt up and out in offering. The man steps closer. Even through the glass, I can feel the air between us thicken.

I spend a few moments luxuriating in the warmth of the water, then turn and squirt some foamy white soap from the dispenser into my hand. I slowly lather my arms, my shoulders. Timidly, my hands fall to my breasts.

I pause. Eyes still half-shrouded, I study myself: the fleshy globes flushed red from the heat, the nipples erect from the pounding spray. My hesitation isn't really an act. At this point in the show I always do wonder—*Can I really do this?*

I really could be a shy virgin exploring the secret pleasures of her own body for the very first time. Inside my head, so many voices clamor and call—*No, it's bad to touch yourself. And worse to do it here, where someone can see you do this naughty thing. You are a dirty, dirty girl.*

But then a husky voice whispers, as warm as the hissing spray—*Do it for me, Jenny-chan. You're not dirty. You're clean and pretty.*

Pretty? Maybe, or at least exotic enough to pass for it here. Clean? I've taken five showers in two hours, but I'm not sure that's the right word for me now. Unless it's become an auto-antonym—a contronym in the linguist's trade—a word that means its own opposite.

These thoughts fill my head, swirling higher like the steam. But I'm not paid to think. The show must go on.

And so, with not quite feigned reluctance, I brush one finger over my cleavage, lingering at the wet crevice. A soft moan escapes my lips.

With a shiver, I pull my hand away and stand with both arms

stiff at my sides. Guiltily, I cast a quick glance to each side, my gaze slipping past the male form shimmering in the haze beyond the glass. My practiced eye takes in my audience in an instant: trousers puddled around ankles, a hand pumping an unremarkable erection with leisurely strokes. He seems to know the best is yet to come. The menu he chose showed a certain familiarity with my services. Perhaps he is a repeat visitor? Or is he here through a referral from a friend?

Either is fine by me. They both tip well.

Swallowing, as if to gather courage, I bring both hands to my breasts and cup them gently. My thumbs find my nipples and I spread the last bits of soap over the tips. Gasping, I rock my hips forward and back, aiming my pubes straight at the glass. My secret admirer lets out a gruff sigh.

My hands glide lower, circling over my belly, dipping between my legs. My finger pushes into my groove, which I've shaved into a modest yet revealing fringe of feminine curls.

Intoxicated by the magic of my own diddling finger, my thighs shake and my knees buckle, but in the next instant I stiffen, as if I've touched a bare wire, trembling from the shock of my own boldness.

Reality is the foundation of every fantasy. Is it true, Hiro, or did *you* make it so?

Because my body really is shaking, my heart pounding like a taiko drum.

I squeeze my eyes closed, letting my face play out the internal struggle. Like a hot, wet, horny virgin, I do want to touch myself in all the naughty places until I'm taken by that sweet clenching in my belly that transports me to a timeless world of ecstasy. In truth, I have indulged in this private pleasure long before I knew a man's caress. There's nothing wrong with it. It's natural and healthy, a proud assertion of my female autonomy and power.

But the voices rise up again. They tell me it's wrong to do this. Wrong to take money to masturbate for strange men in a fantasy sex club in Tokyo, no matter that I sometimes make five thousand dollars a week for a few evenings' work. They tell me I might fool myself that I've stayed clean because I take half a dozen showers a night and have never let a customer so much as touch my hand. But in fact I'm really nothing more than a dirty whore.

You won't be a prostitute, Jenny-chan. No one will touch you, I promise. I'll be watching over you always.

Is Hiro watching now?

My nipples tingle, and I feel a gush of wetness between my thighs. It's not water, no, and it's not for the man jerking off outside the stall. It's for Hiro gazing at me through the hidden surveillance camera.

I squeeze out more soap, rub it over my breasts and push them together as if I'm wearing some obscene bargirl's bustier. It's time to move on to the "Breast Soap Show." I lean forward and press my upper body against the glass. In spite of the heat and steam, the wall itself is cool. Yet, as I rub my nipples against it, the mild sting sends sharper pangs of arousal to my cunt. I shake my shoulders slowly, sliding myself along the hard, slick surface. This is no act. I am genuinely turned on.

And Hiro? Does he feel that chilly fire in his body, too?

A face emerges from the steam, inches from the glass, eyes fixed and bulging. I shimmy faster. A tongue darts out, desperately flicking at the glass. I moan. Hiro's tongue would be just like this, cool and unyielding. He's a cool man in every sense of the word. He never touches his girls, he told me. Mixing work and pleasure dirties things.

But I want to be dirty. I want to be touched. Still moaning, I spread my labia with my fingers and rock my pelvis forward so my pussy is splayed and exposed against the glass. The man cries out and sinks to his knees. He licks me there now, careful catlike flicks at first, but then he grows ardent, pressing his whole tongue against the wall as if he can dissolve the obstacle by sheer effort.

I look down at the man, studying him openly now: the bald spot at the top of his head, the quickening pace of his pumping fist, the plum-colored cockhead ready to burst. All the while I'm grunting, like a woman climbing toward orgasm, although my true desire is more forbidden. I want to look up, through the glass eye of the camera, straight into Hiro's heart.

Suddenly the man stands and aims his tool straight at my pussy. After a few more strokes, three jets of milky spunk spatter the glass. The rest dribbles onto his hand, as he sways with the fading contractions. I wait a few beats so he can enjoy the stunning climax of my own performance. Throwing my head back, I howl and grind my hips against the glass in ersatz frenzy.

Collecting myself, I step back from the glass, my eyes modestly lowered.

But it's not over yet. I time it perfectly. After he's wiped himself with the waiting towels and zipped up, just when he's about to turn his back on me and retreat to the real world, I catch his gaze and smile.

For a moment we are both naked, seen for what we are.

Then, with a quick bow, I step back under the shower and return to my ablutions.

That little smile doubles my tip every time.

Sure enough, when I dry off and check the tray by the door, I've earned two hundred dollars over my cut from the house. The man's left a business card, too, with a one-word message in Japanese.

Kirei.

Clean and pretty. The word means both things in Japanese.

That's what Hiro said to me the first night we met.

I glance up at the camera, just for a moment, and smile.

I'm lounging on the plastic sofa rubbing oil on my skin when the knock comes. I don't bother putting on my robe. I know it's Yuri-chan, the seventyish maid come to clean and replenish the towels for the next round.

As she wipes off the spunk and gives the glass a thorough spray of disinfectant, I continue anointing myself with moisturizer. Otherwise, in this line of work, I'll turn into a prune by week's end.

"Some more tea, Jenny-san? You are working so hard. The boss says you are number one again tonight. No surprise for a pretty girl like you." She flashes me a gold-toothed smile.

I shrug modestly and take the teacup from the tray.

She places a fresh pot beside me with a bow. A steady supply of tea comes in handy for the occasional customer who asks to watch me pee—which somehow seems less perverse in the shower.

Yuri murmurs the standard polite good-byes and bows out of the room.

I'm alone again with my words and my fantasies.

It strikes me that the word *kirei* has a completely different meaning from "clean" or "pretty" in this place. Here it means I keep the money coming in. Pretty is as pretty does.

Out there in the real world, I spend a lot of time thinking about such things: words and the spirit behind them. When I'm not masturbating in the shower for strangers, I'm doing research for my dissertation in comparative linguistics. Hiro pays me twice what my Japan Foundation grant provides.

But he's not exactly the cause of my secret life of degradation. I was leading a secret life for a few months before Hiro found me. It was intellectual curiosity more than money that led me to my first job in the floating world. The "water trade" has a language of its own, and I thought it might add a little spice to my research. Without experience or connections in the business, I had to settle for a downscale position in a high-class strip club. I poured drinks and chatted with customers while the men watched pole dancers reflected in mirrors behind me or, more often, turned to stare at the action with an unmediated eye. Although I was nominally protected by the sturdy bar, I got my share of groping in those first weeks. It made me feel dirty, and I was ready to quit the whole scene when Hiro walked in and changed the course of my career.

Hiro didn't try to touch me, of course. He didn't even gawk at the strippers. Instead he fixed his warm eyes on me and told me in Japanese I was too *kirei* for a place like this. At first I thought he meant I was pretty. But later, when he was treating me to sushi for breakfast at Daiwa in Tsukiji, I knew it was more complicated.

Over the most delicious fatty tuna I'd ever eaten, Hiro explained he'd always been more independent than most Japanese, which was why he felt right at home running fantasy sex clubs for his investor boss. Then he asked me to come work at his new club. He told me it would be very clean, cleaner than what I did at the strip club. He used the word *kirei* for that, too. He promised no one would ever make me dirty. I'd be alone, like in a dream, and in three to six months, I'd wake up much richer, but cleaner than ever.

What could I do but accept his offer? Already I was in love with his graceful hands, his velvet eyes, his deep voice, murmuring.

Kirei.

* * *

Everything happened just as he promised. It's the easiest money I've ever made. Except we're coming up on five months now, and while business is still booming, fads always fade in Japan. Hiro will leave me for another fantasy world, which might involve courtesans from old Japan or Korean court ladies or synchronized swimmers doing acrobatics in tanks in the nude.

Can I let him leave me forever without once breaking through that wall between us?

I glance up at the surveillance camera, then over at the intercom. If I wait here, it will buzz again with news of another customer. Another middle-aged section chief will forget his troubles with a virtual fuck through the glass. Or a threesome of young salarymen will want me to dress up as a mermaid, then strip in the shower while they do a circle jerk, egging each other on with drunken laughter.

Tonight I need something more than this.

My flesh still plumped and tingling from my last encounter, I put on my robe, tie the sash firmly and slip on the sandals the club provides for trips to the toilet. Muffling my footsteps, I creep down the hallway, past the other closed doors where discreet OCCUPIED signs announce that a private show is in progress inside.

The reception area is empty. After the last train to the suburbs, customers slow to a trickle. I slip behind the front desk and glide up to Hiro's office. He's left the door partly open, no doubt to keep watch on the entrance. But he's facing away from the door, his gaze focused on the security monitors, one for each room. I glimpse Kristina doing a mermaid dance for a gray-haired guy, trousers at his knees. Mika-chan kneels, miming fellatio through her shower stall, which is whimsically draped with tropical flowers. Natalie is soaping her breasts under the languid caress of water, but I notice her portly customer must have ordered a blindfold, because a wet scarf is tied fast over her eyes.

But I realize Hiro is not watching them at all. His gaze is fixed on the lower right screen—mine—which should be blank, but isn't. Instead I see my double standing under the too-familiar shower. My eyes are closed, and I'm rubbing myself between my legs.

For a moment I feel dizzy, disoriented. There are too many eyes here. I'm watching Hiro watch a stranger watch me slide my soapy genitals over the glass. Only then do I notice his right arm jerking in an odd motion. I step closer and peer over his shoulder. Hiro's fly is open, his ruddy erection pokes up through his jeans, nestled in his clenched fist. His other hand holds a wad of tissues at the ready. Suddenly he stops.

I freeze. I've been caught spying and will surely pay a price.

But Hiro doesn't seem to see me. He merely reaches over and rewinds the tape. Again I arch back under the spray, my hands wandering timidly down to my breasts. Hiro begins to tug in earnest. He is close.

That silken rope around my chest pulls tight again, but this time the pain is sweet. I have already touched him, and I know just what to do next.

Without a word, I walk into the office and cross in front of the monitors, blocking his view. He starts in surprise, cock still in his hand. The wad of tissues falls to the floor. I bow quickly and murmur an apology for disturbing him, but before he can reply, I untie my robe, pull it over my shoulders and kneel between his legs.

Only then do I meet his eyes.

Our bodies still haven't made the slightest contact, but something has broken between us. There is no glass wall now.

His gaze melts into me with naked longing. My pussy clenches and drools, coating my thighs with my juices. My nipples stiffen to sharp points in the cool air, and my breath comes in gasps. The heat in his eyes fuels a throbbing deep in my cunt, all of those hours of heat and steam compressed into one aching knot of yearning. Just one more caress and he'll send me over the edge. We both know what that will be. Like a film on fast-forward I can already feel the first arcing spurt sizzle into my flesh, smell the grassy ripeness of his cream, see my own hands massaging it over my nipples and dipping slick fingers between my lips to take in the very essence of his desire.

I thrust my shoulders back, offering my breasts, my neck, my face.

Kirei ni shite.

Make me clean. And pretty. And dirty. And very, very rich.

He begins to pump, faster, his mouth twisting into a grimace.

I tilt my head back, lips parted, thirsty for the first pulses of that hot shower on my skin.

SUPERIOR

Monica Shores

The package was small, and you trembled a bit as you thrust it into my hands. Such shyness would have seemed strange in a man so tall if it wasn't one of your defining traits. You bowed your head slightly.

"Happy Valentine's Day," you managed, your fingers colliding with my own.

"And to you," I said, momentarily caught off guard. Everyone else had left and I assumed you had too when I began gathering my coat and files to take home. But then there you were in front of me, offering me this gift. You smiled and met my gaze for an instant—I'd forgotten your eyes were blue since you showed them to me so rarely—and just as suddenly as you appeared you were gone, out my door and down the hall.

I returned to my desk and set down my things, loosening the wrapping paper with one fingernail. As soon as I felt the sheer fabric, I knew it was panty hose. They were Wolford's and they were my size.

Of course I knew you wanted me, but I hadn't expected this. You weren't the first assistant who hid his hard-on when called into my office. Was there ever a time you didn't blush when I said your name? I grew to love watching you lower your legal pad over your crotch as you lowered your eyes away from my cleavage, down to my perpetually stocking-clad legs. It was as though you'd never seen a woman in microfishnets before.

I took in a deep breath and exhaled slowly before rebooting my computer. I was your boss. I couldn't let something like this go unaddressed. With an email open and addressed to you, I wrote simply, *Be at Blacksalt, 9 p.m. tomorrow.* It would be Saturday, February 14th and I was certain that if you had plans, you would break them.

I idly drew a drink straw back and forth over my lips as I sat at the bar, swiveling the stem of the glass with my middle finger and thumb. It was only 8:30, but I knew you'd be early. I was wearing a thin crepe blouse, deep red with a low neckline, an ivory wool miniskirt, and your panty hose. My toned legs looked irresistible in the black stockings; every man at the bar had already eyed them hungrily as I sipped my sidecar and returned their stares.

As expected, I spotted your lanky frame just moments later when you came through the door, cheeks red from the wind as you swept your fingers through your hair to smooth it down. Once you saw me, I turned away and placed my hand on the knee of the man next to me.

I'd chosen him immediately. He had thick, ringless hands, an arrogant air, and the slightly paunchy belly of someone who spoils himself. We exchanged only one charged glance before he bought me my drink. Our small talk had gone stale minutes ago; he was eager for things to get interesting and I was eager to give you a show.

Your eyes were on my back as I reached up to push my dark hair off of my shoulders, showing my pale neck to you, the man, and anyone else who was looking. I fingered the cloth of his pants and tilted my head to the side, watching you approach from the corner of my eye.

"So, you're spending Valentine's Day alone? Is that by choice or by circumstance?"

You slid into a booth next to the door, catty-corner to us, never taking your eyes from me.

"Both," the man replied, tipping some of his scotch down his throat. "But I can tell that for you, it's all choice."

"That's right," I said, turning my body on the stool so that my knees wouldn't block your view of my hand as it crept up his thigh. I could feel wetness welling up between my legs, not from touching him but from feeling your anguished gaze. "I can be alone or I can have company. But you could have company, too. I know a place we can go that's just around the corner."

"And what place is that?" he asked. Glass empty, he set his heavy hand on my leg, on your panty hose, sliding his hot palm halfway up my thigh. A waitress momentarily blocked your view of us before you hurried her away with a terse drink order.

I beckoned him forward and leaned to whisper in his ear. For the first time, my eyes fully met yours. Your expression was pained as you looked back and forth between my face and the man's hand. I imagined your cock stiffening as you watched him rub my leg, and that thought sent a surge to my pussy that made my eyelids lower.

"My office." I angled my mouth so you could see my lips move as I drew out the words: "I've always wanted to fuck on my desk."

"Then what are we waiting for?" he asked, smiling, finally sliding his hand all the way up until his fingers brushed my cunt.

He squeezed the soft flesh of my uppermost inner thigh and then he withdrew, dragging his blunt fingertips down the length of my leg. You sputtered and coughed violently, setting down the drink you had just lifted to your lips.

I slipped my fingers into his as he tossed some bills onto the rail and we started toward the door. Outside, I pulled him into a walk so quick that it was almost a jog and began giving him instructions. I had heard you scrambling to pay and leave; I knew you wouldn't be far behind us.

"You'll have to wait for me at the back entrance because there's a security guard at the front," I lied, raising my free hand to point as we approached the building. "Just follow the sidewalk here and you'll see a little alleyway in the back. There's a door right there."

"Don't keep me waiting," he leered as I veered away from him toward the front doors.

I punched in the entry code and flew through the lobby. You had the code, too, and you wouldn't be far behind. I had just enough time to throw on the lights, slide into my chair, and smooth my skirt before you were there.

You appeared in the doorway like someone had pushed you forward, off balance and wild eyed, out of breath. "Where's…I thought—" You scanned the room, baffled, then looked to me for some explanation.

"What are you doing here?" I asked with an edge in my voice. Cruel. I curled my fingers around the ends of the chair arms, holding my spine straight.

"I wasn't sure I could stand it, but I had to see." You stumbled forward as you searched my face for some encouragement. I could tell you were at once relieved and disappointed to see me alone. Your panic made you forget to be shy.

"See what?"

"You!" Your face nearly crumpled in frustration. You made a move as though to reach out to me, then checked yourself. Your hand fell to your side. "You, even if you were…with someone else. I had to see it. You."

"Why?" I leaned forward. My legs felt so sleek in those hose that just the drag of fabric against my calves as I uncrossed my legs made my pussy pulse. "Tell me exactly why."

"Because." You took a deep breath. I locked my eyes on yours and saw a small shudder pass through your body before you blurted out: "Because I can't stop thinking about you. Because I bought a dozen pairs of panty hose before I got up the nerve to give you one. Because I jerk off to the thought of you every night and I don't care what it means anymore, I have to—"

"Be quiet." I said. Your jaw was clenched and your eyes were flashing. This was the most you'd ever said to me at one time. My pussy was throbbing because of your desperation. Just seeing your nostrils flare was enough to keep me going. "Take off your pants."

You looked at me, your face falling as distress dissolved into something like fear. I watched the crotch of your pants swell steadily and again you made a move, this time as if to shield your hard-on from view. Your cheeks were a hot red, and I noticed that the hair against your forehead and temples was curled wet with sweat.

"I won't say it again. Your boxers, too."

You pulled off your shoes and fumbled with your belt until your trousers were dropped and kicked to the side. Under your shirttails, your cock was hard and drowsing out toward me, sleek and long. It had a sharp upward curve and a prominent head with a shiny, defined ridge. I wanted to put my mouth on it, but instead I said:

"Start jerking it for me."

You closed your hand around your dick tentatively, as though the motion was unfamiliar. But as I stared, you began stroking up and down slowly. Because your skin was dry, there was friction, and the slight drag of your cock's skin against your palm made every move seem more deliberate and firm.

"You think you can get hard at work without any consequences?" I pressed my hands to my inner thighs and began caressing the silk and soft skin underneath as I reclined in the chair. I felt my nipples stiffening as I matched the pace of my strokes with your own. "You thought you would just give me a gift and suddenly I'd find you irresistible? That I'd kiss you in gratitude? Or that I'd put on these panty hose for you in the office after hours? That I'd straddle your lap while wearing them?"

You shook your head and bit your lip, dropping your eyes from mine as you blushed even more painfully red. Shame almost seemed to embolden you, and you jerked more harshly with each word. Your cock had become glossy with precome, which frothed steadily from the tip.

"Take off your shirt," I said, reaching for my own buttons. "Then keep going."

Your fingers shook as you unbuttoned your shirt. The chest you revealed was broad and flat with a trail of curly black hair leading from your belly button down to your cock, which bounced a bit as you tossed the shirt to the side. Your arms were more muscled than I expected, your biceps hard and your shoulders strong. My fingers loosened my own buttons as I watched, stripping off my blouse in time with you. You wrapped your fingers around your dick and started pulling at it again with long, tight strokes, occasionally flipping your wrist so you could tug underhanded. The more embarrassed you became, the more confidant you seemed as you touched yourself.

I hiked my skirt up around my hips so you could fully see your gift. My groomed pubic hair lay flat underneath the fabric above the beginning of the reinforced oval that covered my cunt. I wasn't wearing underwear, and my outer pussy lips pressed against the taut mesh. I drew my fingers over the hair before tracing them down around the oval's seams. My wetness was seeping through, and had been since you first kicked off your pants. I glanced up to see your eyes glued to my hands. Your body almost seemed to struggle against itself as you writhed from the sensation of your palm's skin over the head of your cock.

"Are you getting what you want?" I mocked softly. "Is this just what you imagined? Or did you think I'd be begging you to fuck me?"

You turned your head away, exposing the tendons in your smooth neck. Your nipples were stiff and the defined muscles of your stomach flexed and released in time with your strokes. Just watching your body tense was enough to send another wave of heat through my cunt, and I hooked my right leg over the arm of the chair.

"Look at me," I said, and you did, eyes blazing with frustrated lust.

"Were you this hard in the restaurant?" I lifted my other leg and you let out a low moan. My pussy was swollen and slick, my juices saturating the panty hose. My fingers were coated.

"Yes. The whole time," you panted, convulsing with pleasure as you began pumping your hips back and forth, moving your cock into your fist like you were fucking a pussy.

"Because you liked seeing me with another man."

"No—yes. I don't know. I wanted to be him." You stopped and squeezed the base of your cock, trembling. Your balls were tight and high, ready to explode. It made me wetter to see you struggling not to come, and I squirmed, stretching my inner thighs and moving my fingers more rapidly over the oval.

"But you aren't him," I said, trying to control my own breathing. My free hand toyed with my left nipple through the lace of my bra until I pulled the fabric aside in impatience, baring my tit. "So you were just going to watch. Maybe you'll only ever get to watch."

I lifted the panty hose's waistband and slid my hand underneath. My fingers immediately found my hot hole and plunged inside. I felt the deep, shallow shudders of a near-orgasm and I gasped, willing myself not to tip over the edge. I pulled out for a moment before reaching back in. I couldn't bear not to be filled as I watched you beat off.

"Come here," I said breathily, while my fingers slithered in and out. Nearly all pretense of stern self-control was gone. I wriggled lewdly against the seat of the chair and the greasy skin of my own hand. "Stand between my ankles. Keep stroking." I split my legs even farther as you came toward me, jerking unevenly as you tried to restrain yourself. Your hand stopped just before the head, concentrating only on the raw, red shaft.

"Tell me what you want." I looked down at the dark tangled hair of your love trail and your clenched fist as it alternately hid and exposed your swollen cockhead. My clit was huge, and I twitched as the ball of my hand rocked over it while I finger-fucked my drenched cunt. I glanced up at your face, and saw that you were staring down through the transparent black hose and the soaked white oval, your mouth open and eyes glazed.

"Oh god," you muttered. "I want to be inside you. I want to hear you moan while you squirm and roll your hips."

"What else do you want?" I tilted my pelvis forward, rotating my pussy downward and pushing my clit out even more. I slipped a third finger inside and moaned. My tunnel was pulpy with juice, and I squeezed down, pulsing my muscles around my fingers. I could smell myself and you could, too. Every few breaths, you inhaled deeply through your nose, eyes rolling back.

"I want to feel you come on my cock," you groaned. "I want you screaming and grinding on me and using me to get off over and over. I want to watch your face when you come. But I want you to blindfold me and tell me that I can't. I want my thighs to be smeared with you. I want you to pull my hair and slap my face and make me finish in my own hand."

"What else?" My tongue licked my lips as I stared at the gaping tip of your dick. I had never seen a man with so much precome. It was smeared all over your shaft and clinging to your pubic hair.

"I want to lick you through those panty hose. I want to suck your wetness out of them when you're done. I want you to tie them on me like a gag and suck me off and then spit my come back into my mouth. I want the scent of you all over my face."

Then I reached out with my left hand and touched your face, just barely. My fingertips brushed your sweaty temple before sliding into your thick black hair, twining through the strands and pulling your face closer to mine. Your cock wasn't touching me, but it was so close that I felt the heat of it, and the slight breeze as your fist pumped back and forth.

I knew all of this already. Of course you wanted me to hit you and ride you and make you eat your own come. You wanted me to rub my panty hose–covered feet all over your chest and cock until you came on my toes. You wanted me to get you off under the table of a crowded restaurant, or in a bar, or in a car while you drove us through the city streets. But you weren't telling me what you really wanted. You didn't have to, though; I already knew that too. You wanted me to call your name.

"Julian," I whispered thickly against your ear.

You came instantly, hard, gasping and twitching as you spattered my belly and the stretched mesh, wetting my wrist. You heaved forward into me, moaning with the final few strokes, and I watched as you milked out the last hot, pearly drops. I pressed my lips into your neck so you could feel my smile and you let out an incredulous half pant, half laugh, collapsing to your knees in front of me.

"Julian," I said again. I drew my face back so I could look fully into your eyes, still holding your head. Your grin was huge and this time you didn't look away. Instead, you lunged for my mouth, and I opened for your tongue. As you chewed at my lower lip, I drew my slick fingers out from between my legs and pushed them into your mouth. You sucked greedily, immediately, and your hand began moving up my thigh. But I stopped you.

It was your turn to watch.

PEOPLE IN GLASS HOTELS

Jennifer Peters

There's something about traveling far from home that always makes me a little more outgoing. Sometimes I think it's because the chances are slim of ever running into the people who've witnessed my most outrageous acts, and that's definitely a part of it, but I think the real reason our trips make me so bold is that I love sharing that secret side of me with a whole new audience.

I feel like a rock star on a world tour, playing for a new crowd each night, the set list never getting old because there're always new ears to take in what could easily be considered the same old sounds. But instead of rocking out onstage with an electric guitar, I can be found fucking my brains out on my own makeshift stage, giving my audience a better show than any rock band could.

It all started when I was in college and my friends and I would travel all over the country on spring break. Our first trip was to San Francisco, and while most of my group was touring

Alcatraz or hanging out at Fisherman's Wharf, I was busy in the hotel room with my boyfriend. It wasn't until halfway through our ten-day trip that Emmett and I finally ventured farther from the hotel than the diner around the corner, and being outside the room was driving me crazy. All I wanted to do was climb back into bed with him and go back to our much more private activities. Our friends wouldn't stand for it, though, and I was forced to endure hours of "fun" as we toured the city.

Late in the afternoon, a group of us decided to make the trek to the Golden Gate Bridge, and, I must admit, I was looking forward to seeing the architectural marvel up close. I'd watched so many documentaries about its construction that I was willing to sacrifice some of my alone time with Emmett in order to test its strength and take a few photos to savor later.

The bridge at sunset was gorgeous—and arousing. By the time we were ready to start walking back to our hotel, I was feeling incredibly horny. Emmett seemed to be feeling the same urges I was, constantly pulling me closer to him and kissing me over and over again, even though he hated public displays of affection. The more he kissed me and touched me, the hotter it made me, and by the time we were halfway down the hill from the bridge, I was ready to jump Emmett.

We were on the same page again, and when we passed a deserted picnic table in a fairly overgrown area, we slowed to the back of our group, pretending to be admiring the bridge from afar. When everyone had passed us, we raced over to the abandoned table and I sat down on the warped wooden tabletop before pulling Emmett down with me. It took us only a few moments to undo zippers and buttons and tug open shirts and pants just enough to reach inside, and then we were fucking frantically, our usually casual lovemaking thrown out the window in our quest for instant gratification. It was awkward and hurried, but fantastic all the same, and the prospect of being caught at any moment had my heart beating wildly, in the best way possible.

It was over almost as soon as it began, but it sparked an entirely new desire in me. From that moment on, I wanted to search out the riskiest locations for encounters with Emmett, and the boyfriends that followed. Something about being out in the open and the possibility of having strangers "catch me" in the middle of such a private moment made my heart race and my pussy tingle. From bathrooms to barrooms, kitchens to conference rooms, I dragged dates to every single public place I could think of that would allow for private—but incredibly risky—moments of coupling.

I wasn't nearly as daring as I thought, however, and aside from someone overhearing us in a bathroom and turning around to leave, or a friend walking in on us and then bolting, I never seemed to get caught. This was, for the most part, all right with me—until I met Felix.

Felix and I were introduced by mutual friends and we hit it off immediately. We had similar values and morals, the same sense of humor and the kinds of busy schedules that made it hard to date. When we discovered that we had an equally intense sexual chemistry, we knew we were it for each other.

Felix loves to show off, whether it's winning at board games, impressing the boss during a meeting or fucking for an audience, letting the world know of his sexual prowess. When we first met, he was far more adventurous than I was, and whenever he'd pull me aside for a secret rendezvous, we'd always get caught. While I opted for spaces with doors and a semblance of privacy, like restrooms or dark, hidden alleyways behind even darker bars, Felix preferred much more open spaces, like in a hotel pool with others swimming nearby, crowded airplanes—and I don't mean in the bathrooms—or under the bleachers during one of his summer softball games. And we always had witnesses, usually several at a time, from fellow passengers, flight attendants, and vacationing businessmen to our coworkers and friends—who probably witnessed our escapades more times than they liked.

When we decided to get married, I was determined to show him that I could be as out-there as he was, and I begged him to let me plan the last weekend of our honeymoon in Germany. He'd already planned most of the three-week trip already, but he was happy to hand me the reins when it came to planning our time in Berlin.

I already knew exactly where we'd be staying and what we'd be doing—and it had nothing to do with the city's many tourist stops. In preparation for our trip, I'd been watching the Travel Channel nonstop, making sure not to miss a single program if it mentioned Germany. During one of my marathon viewing sessions, I came across a show called "Passport to Europe," and I just so happened to catch it on the day the host was visiting Berlin. The city, which I'd never been to before, was beautiful, but it wasn't the historic or tourist sites that caught my attention. What really drew me in was the hotel they featured.

Located in the heart of Berlin, the Velvet Hotel was a modern luxury hotel that had every amenity I could hope for. The restaurant was classy, the service seemed to be top-notch, the price was right and the rooms were gorgeous. It was also an exhibitionist's dream come true. The outside wall of each room was a giant window, the width and height of the room, and gave a great view of the city—and gave the city a great view of the rooms. While the host prattled on about admiring the city at night, all I could think about was having the people of Berlin admiring Felix and me.

For weeks leading up to our wedding and honeymoon, I

found myself constantly daydreaming about our weekend in the Velvet Hotel. I imagined all the things we could do and how many people would be watching us. I envisioned the crowd that would appear while we made love, our bed right next to the window. Or maybe Felix would take me from behind, fucking me hard while my breasts pressed up against the cool glass of the window. I'd get so lost in my fantasies that I'd end up getting horny while reading travel books or watching the dozens of Travel Channel programs I'd saved on our DVR. I constantly masturbated, my fingers idly playing with my pussy as I worked on planning our trip. Other times, I'd sit down at the computer with my vibrator and let it buzz deep inside my aching cunt while I looked at the hotel's website, the exterior photos exciting me more than any of the real porn my husband liked to bring home. I'd never been so turned on in my life, and it was all over a silly hotel. It excited me so much that I was in a constant state of arousal, and I feared my fiancé would grow suspicious. Luckily, Felix never found out about my travel porn, and I was able to keep secret our planned rendezvous at the Velvet Hotel, though I did have to buy a few replacement travel guides, their tattered predecessors hidden in the bedside drawer where I kept my vibrators and lubes.

When our wedding—and subsequent honeymoon—finally rolled around, I was more than ready to take off with my new husband. I still had to wait a few weeks to get to Berlin, though, and I wasn't sure I could keep the secret much longer.

After weeks of my fantasizing, we arrived in Berlin. Our first stop was, of course, our hotel, and when we were standing in front of the grand building, my husband couldn't stop staring up at the hundreds of windows—and neither could any of the passersby on the street. Not a single person walked past without glancing up at the elaborate glass hotel, and my heart started racing as I imagined them looking up at those same windows once Felix and I were inside. What would they see? Would they stop and stare, or pretend they were unaffected and keep walking? I could feel my pussy tingling with each thought, and I knew I had to get my husband inside immediately and put my plan into action or I'd come right there on the sidewalk.

Felix was too surprised—too turned on, really—to help with the check-in, but the second I tipped the bellman and closed the door to our room, he was right there, pulling me into his arms and kissing me wildly. It appeared he was pleased.

"What is this place?" he asked, his breathing ragged and his eyes shining with lust.

"A hotel," I replied, doing my best to keep a straight face.

"You know what, never mind. I don't care," he said, and then he was pulling me to him again, attacking my mouth with his own.

His kisses were hungry and demanding, and when his tongue begged permission to enter my mouth, I eagerly allowed it, my own tongue darting forward to welcome him. From the corner of my eye, I could see the light pouring into our third-floor room through the window, and it excited me even more. I became more aggressive, pulling Felix tight against my body and hooking a leg around his waist. I could feel his arousal through his pants, and I knew I had to get us over to the window before we wasted perfectly good sex on a private room.

Dropping my leg from his waist, I started leading my husband away from the door and closer to the window. When we reached the bed, he broke our lip-lock momentarily and started to turn toward the bed, but even though I knew the bed was, for the most part, visible from the street, I wanted to be right up against the glass. The thought of fucking him against the smooth surface, of being completely on display, had been making me wet for weeks on end and I wasn't going to settle for anything less now that we were finally in my dream hotel.

When we were standing right in front of the wall of glass, I held Felix's hand tightly and turned to stare out the window for a moment. The city really was beautiful, and I could see why people—even those who weren't exhibitionists—wanted to stay at the Velvet Hotel. Of course, when I looked down and saw dozens of people on the street in front of our hotel, all of them pausing to look up into the windows when they passed the spectacular building, I remembered why *I* wanted to stay there, too.

Turning back to my husband, I said, "We're a bit overdressed for this afternoon's activities," and Felix immediately jumped into action and began tugging at my shirt and his pants, unsure of who to undress first. I laughed briefly at his excitement and then got to work helping him, unbuttoning his shirt and undoing his belt while he tried to remove my own clothing as quickly as possible.

As shirts were torn off, I felt my pulse speed up a bit. When pants and shoes were kicked away a moment later and our lips joined in a hot kiss, I felt my pussy start to throb, moisture already leaking out into my thong. And when panties and boxers were tossed aside and we were both left standing naked in the window, I came. I had yet to touch or be touched, and while our kiss was passionate, it wasn't quite that heated. No, the thought of all those tourists looking up and seeing me naked in the window, my husband standing in front of me, his cock erect, well, the thought had been too much for me. It set me off, making me moan in pleasure while my juices flooded my pussy in anticipation of the next step.

Felix made the next move, and before I could look away from the glass, he'd pushed me up against it. My breasts were flattened against the cool, smooth surface, and when I looked down, I could see several people looking back up at me—or at least I told myself they were all looking at me; it was hard to tell which window had captured their attention, and I was a bit distracted. I sighed as I stared down at them, and then Felix was pressing his body against mine, his stiff dick nestling between my asscheeks as he kissed my neck and ran his hands up and down my body, eventually wrapping his arms around me and letting his hands wander down toward my pussy. When a finger brushed my wet pussy lips, I moaned and pressed my forehead against the window, my eyes closed tight. When I opened them, however, there were still people staring up at me. And this time I was sure it was me they were watching, because the handful of people from a minute earlier were still there and were now joined by others, some of them pointing up at the window.

"They're watching us," I breathlessly told Felix, and he mumbled something in my ear that sounded a lot like, "No, they're watching *you*," though his voice was so rough with passion that it was hard to make out his exact words.

Part of me wanted to drag out the experience, make it last as long as possible; tease the audience, Felix, myself; but a bigger part was so turned on by the scene we were creating that I wanted to dive right in. We had three more days for slow and sensual, after all, and I needed Felix to fuck me right that minute or else I'd go crazy with desire.

Reaching back, I grabbed his cock and stroked it several times, letting him know what I wanted without saying a word. He responded quickly, pulling my hips back from the window and positioning me so that I could still look out while he took me from behind. I'm pretty sure he wanted to gaze at our audience, too, and I couldn't blame him. The thought of dozens of strangers watching while he had his way with me created the most natural high, and I couldn't deny my husband the same pleasure.

With one swift, strong thrust, he entered me, pushing my chest even harder against the window. My moans were creating fog on the glass and my sweaty breasts were leaving their marks as well, but for me it all added to the show we were putting on, made our actions more real for the curious onlookers, proving we were not some sanitized porn stars or worse, faking it.

Almost immediately, Felix started pumping in and out of my soaked pussy. For the first few strokes, I was too busy watching the people on the street below to pay attention to what I was feeling, but when he started moving faster, his flesh slapping against my own, I got lost in the sensations he was creating, the tingles traveling from my pussy to the rest of my body. I almost forgot about our growing audience—almost, but not completely. The entire time Felix was pounding my pussy—expertly, I might add—at least a small part of my mind was focused on the people in the street who were watching us. I wondered what they were thinking and who they thought we were. I wished I had the ability to read minds so that I could find out who down there was turned on by us, who was embarrassed to be watching, who wanted it to be them up in our room, fucking for all to see.

My imagination was running wild again, like it had when I'd been planning our stay, but now it was even more graphic because I had so many visuals to work with. I was no longer imagining only Felix and me making love with some faceless stick figures watching us. Now I knew what our audience looked like, and I began envisioning them cheering for us, clapping wildly when we came. I even imagined a few of them trading places with us, them up in the room making love for all to see while Felix and I stood down below, staring up with lust in our eyes.

The feelings were becoming too intense for me—and my

husband, too, who was grunting and moaning loudly, the way he does just before he comes.

"I'm going to come!" I cried out, my pussy spasming wildly as soon as the words left my mouth. I writhed against the glass, smearing sweat all over the otherwise crystal-clear window. It was the most intense orgasm I'd ever experienced, and all I wanted to do afterward was collapse in bed with Felix and relive our show in my dreams. But when he announced his own release a moment later, I knew there was one last thing I had to do before I could rest.

As I felt my husband's dick begin to twitch between my legs, I shifted slightly, his cock popping free of my pussy. Then I grabbed it with my right hand and began jerking him off, not stopping until he'd exploded, shooting all over a pristine area of glass. The sight set me off again, and after one more intense climax, I dragged Felix over to the bed and we fell onto it in a sweaty heap.

I know we weren't the first couple to have sex in a hotel window, and we won't have been the last, but I like to think we did it best. At least until we find a way to top our stay at the Velvet Hotel.

INDECENT

Lolita Lopez

Tummy aquiver with anticipation, Trini pressed her back against the stone wall and inhaled a steadying breath. The coolness of the stone seeped through the thin turquoise fabric of her skimpy jacket. Balmy evening air kissed her cheeks. Gulping nervously, she pulled the white cotton gloves from her waistband and slipped her fingers inside. She tugged the ivory half-mask down over her forehead and across her nose. An elastic band held it snugly against her face. Trini plunked the flamboyant top hat onto her head and made sure it was pulled down tight. Her fingers danced across the oversized 10/6 price tag tacked onto the left side.

From down below came the soft hum of excited voices. Energized by the sounds of the milling crowd, Trini smoothed her palms over the black shorts clinging to her derriere and barely skimming her upper thighs. A tiny smile curved her lips. It was now or never.

Summoning all her courage, Trini punched the PLAY button

on the boom box sitting on the ledge. A second later the brassy intro of Joe Cocker's "You Can Leave Your Hat On" filtered through the speakers. Cheers and whistles erupted from below. They knew what was coming.

With the grace of a gymnast, Trini vaulted onto the wide ledge of the Academic Building's roof, her bare soles balancing on the rough stone. At the sight of Trini in her sexy Mad Hatter getup, the crowd of coeds went wild. A thrill of excitement rippled through her body. Trini lived for the adrenaline rush stripping in public provided. Every semester for the past four years, she'd carefully planned these little illicit displays of exhibitionism, dropping discreet clues around campus and on various online networking sites. With each daring escapade, her audience grew. Tonight, her final show at the university, the level of interest didn't disappoint. At a glance, Trini estimated triple her last crowd.

Of course, the popularity brought its own risks, namely quicker discovery by the campus police. But as an applied mathematics major, Trini easily calculated the odds of evasion and capture. She planned her stripteases down to the very last second and studied the various escape routes and their odds of success. Besides, the thrill of the chase only heightened the post-show orgasm with which she'd later gift herself as a reward.

Hips sensually swinging, Trini lowered herself into a wide-legged crouch and then slowly rose to full stature. She flung her top hat into the crowd before carefully turning and shaking her tight ass for the crowd's delight. Her fingers worked the loose knot of her garish yellow and turquoise tie. Facing the crowd again, she let the tie flutter toward the ground. Trini grasped the exaggerated lapels of her jacket and spread the fabric wide, showing off her glittery gold push-up bra and tan tummy. The jacket sleeves whisked down her arms. She twirled the jacket overhead before launching it into the crowd.

Like a belly dancer, she slowly gyrated while running her palms over the full curves of her breasts and along the gentle slope of her rib cage. Her fingers danced across her belly and hooked into the sides of her skimpy black shorts. With a forceful tug, Trini broke the Velcro side seams and crotch. Excited cheers and whistles resounded. A group of frat boys fought over the fabric scraps raining down upon them.

Trini strutted confidently along the ledge, showing off her gleaming, toned legs and the shockingly scant swatch of gold material covering her immaculately waxed sex. A cool breeze buffeted her body, highlighting the dampness of the material pressed up against her cunt and hidden between the cheeks of her ass. Her body hummed with arousal, feeding off the vibrant energy of the crowd. The hardened peaks of her breasts poked against the thin material constraining them. Trini wanted nothing more than to slip her fingers beneath her G-string and strum her stiff clit.

But it wouldn't take much to send her hurling over the edge—literally and figuratively.

Always careful, Trini balanced her sensual dance moves with the utmost caution. One wrong step and she'd tumble five stories. The injuries she might survive, but the humiliation of having her identity discovered would be an injury beyond convalescence. She doubted MIT would be very keen to enroll and fund a grad student embroiled in such a scandal at her previous school. And yet Trini couldn't stop herself. The risk heightened the allure.

A quick flick unsnapped the front closure of her bra, freeing her breasts to the hungry eyes of those gathered below. Tiny painted renditions of the university's logo concealed her nipples and areolas. Arms clasped in front, Trini hopped and wiggled, giving the crowd exactly what they wanted. Her bouncing breasts and jiggling ass incensed them. They hooted and hollered and whistled and begged for more.

Never one to disappoint, Trini turned her back on them and started to bend forward, granting them an exceptional view of her pert ass. Fingers on the waistband of her G-string, she prepared to teasingly remove her panties. She couldn't wait to see the boys and girls below fight over them.

"COPS! COPS!"

Trini snapped to attention. Down below, the crowd scattered in a noisy panic. Not wasting a second, Trini leapt to the roof, slapped the stop button on the boom box, grabbed her backpack and jammed the stereo down inside. She fled toward the door and paused just long enough to snatch up the small wood wedge propping the door open before racing into the narrow stairwell. The door slammed behind her as she stuffed the wood into the slight opening in her backpack. She sprinted down the first two flights of stairs, swinging herself around the sharp corners, her gloves sliding against the metal rails.

Flashlight beams ricocheted around the stairwell a few floors down. Trini immediately stopped and headed back up to the fourth floor. She quietly opened the door and held it against her fingertips as she gently closed it behind her. Safe inside the hallway lined with administrative offices, Trini sprinted along the corridor, her bare feet slapping against rough commercial carpet.

Her mind reeled as she tried to work out her best course of action now that the campus cops were hot on her heels. Routes one through three were out of the question. That left her with one choice. Trini's hand dove into her backpack and frantically fished for the polyester lanyard. She jerked it out and skidded to a halt in front of the first door she reached, not caring whose office it was. Trini tried to jab the master key she'd nicked a few semesters back into the lock. It wouldn't fit.

"Shit! Fuck!" Trini's irritated whisper pierced the stillness. Refusing to waste any more time, she moved to the next door. Again, the key proved useless. It appeared the locks had been changed since her theft of the key.

Trini glanced around anxiously. She spotted the main staircase heading back up to the fifth floor. It was her only chance. She couldn't go back down since the fuzz was sure to have cordoned off all the exits. If she could just get upstairs, she might be able to find some place to hide. Hopefully. Maybe.

As she made a mad dash for the stairs, Trini couldn't quash the grin tugging at the corners of her mouth. A hysterical laugh tickled the back of her throat. Bizarre as it sounded, she actually enjoyed the real sense of danger. Had everything gone as planned, it would have been exciting. *This* was exhilarating. All her well-laid plans were going to hell in a handbasket. The threat of capture was a reality. Rather perversely, she found that invigorating.

Taking the steps two at a time, Trini tried to outpace the cops she could hear thundering up the stairs, not far behind. Hoping for a break, she tried every doorknob she passed, praying just one person had forgotten to lock his door at the end of a long workday. Her gaze darted from side to side, desperately searching for a hiding place. Even with all the furniture and potted plants decorating the floor housing the university president's office, there were no options.

Suddenly, the door to the president's office jerked open. A pair of arms shot out of the darkened room and wound around Trini's waist. She stifled a shocked scream, unwilling to alert the police to her position even as the stranger dragged her into the office. A hand clapped over her mouth. The door closed. An unseen hand locked it from the inside.

"Don't make any noise, Trini."

Trini recognized the Australian accent. Her clamoring pulse slowed just a bit. But what was Dr. Menzies doing in the president's office? His office was halfway across campus in the bowels of the physics department's main building. And, more importantly, how the hell did he know it was her?

He palmed her waist and spun her around. Trini's breasts rasped against the stiff cotton and hard buttons of his shirt as he pressed her back to the door. She gasped at the cold sensation of the wood against her hot, sweat-slicked skin. Trapped there, between his lean body and the door and the cops searching the building, she felt only the thrill of danger and not the fear. She flushed with desire and excitement.

When his fingers skimmed her face and traced her jaw, Trini gulped with apprehension. The room was dark but the slatted blinds allowed just enough moonlight and ambient light to cast a silvery haze of illumination. Through the slits of her mask, their gazes clashed, his pale blue irises against her deep brown ones. His blond hair looked carelessly mussed, framing his incredibly handsome face with boyish loose curls.

He whisked away the mask and dropped it to the floor. Trini's tummy flip-flopped at the sensation of his fingertips caressing her face. His thumb moved across her lower lip, pulling it down gently; a fingertip grazed her teeth. A shock of heat pierced Trini's chest.

There it was: that spark of attraction Trini had experienced all those months earlier when they'd first been introduced by her mathematics mentor. As a professor of theoretical physics, Dr. Menzies often utilized undergrads from the math department in his research. They'd worked together for a semester, a stretch of weeks where Trini found it increasingly difficult to deny her raging lust for him. She often imagined he felt the same. There were too many accidental touches, too many endearing smiles, and too much teasing banter.

And now here they were, pressed belly to belly, pulses pounding, gazes locked.

"How, Dr. Menzies?" Trini asked, finally daring to break the silence.

An impish grin played at his lips. He bent his head and ghosted his lips across the small cluster of scars along her collarbone. She'd earned those as a freshman in high school when her dolt of a lab partner had blown up a test tube. Scorching glass shards had made easy work of penetrating her T-shirt and tearing into her skin.

Trini shivered as Dr. Menzies pressed his lips to her ear. "You'd be amazed what detail a person familiar with photo-analyzing algorithms can bring out from grainy pics posted online. And it's Simon now."

Trini smiled, thoroughly impressed with his detective work. He'd probably spotted the scar during one of their evening number-crunching sessions. She'd often worn tank tops with her jeans and bared those scars without much thought as to their ability to identify her. Thank goodness the campus police seemed devoid of any technological proficiency.

She yearned to touch him but her hands still grasped the strap of her backpack. As if sensing her need, Simon took the bag from her hand and gently set it aside, careful not to make any noise. He removed the gloves encasing her hands and dropped them too. For a long moment, they simply stared at one another. Unable to contain her lust, Trini pounced on him. Simon groaned into her mouth, his tongue searching for hers. The ensuing kisses weren't particularly dignified or finessed but hungry and sloppy and desperate. They clutched and groped, Trini's fingers fumbling with the buttons of his shirt, Simon's hands kneading her breasts, tweaking her nipples.

With a slight shove, Simon pushed Trini's back to the door. He dropped to his knees and grabbed the tiny elastic band of her G-string. As he jerked it down, Trini widened her stance and then lifted her left foot. The G-string remained hooked around her right ankle. Simon's knuckles brushed downward over the bare lips of her pussy. She shivered at the contact.

Without warning, Simon delved into her dripping cunt, swiping the length of her slit with his pointed tongue. Trini stifled a surprised moan, now only vaguely aware of the other voices in the building. Simon clasped the back of her right knee and guided it up and over his shoulder. Trini hooked her left knee in the same way.

Suspended on his shoulders, she sifted her fingers through his soft blond hair and enjoyed his jaw-dropping cunnilingus skills. His thumbs held her open, baring the dewy petals of her sex. He lapped gently at her clit then drifted lower and circled the opening there. When his tongue dipped inside, tasting her, Trini hissed. The velvet sensation of his tongue drawing circles against her inflamed clit made her toes curl. He alternated delicious swirls with pointed flicks and sometimes sucked her pleasure button between his lips, heightening the sensation even more. There was no hesitation or uncertainty from Simon. He ate her cunt with wicked abandon, lavishing every pink inch with attention. Trini's thighs tightened. Her calves flexed against his back. She was going to come—and hard.

Suddenly, a pair of male voices sounded outside the door. Trini expected Simon to pull back, to halt and nervously wait it out, but he didn't. Instead he went wild on her clit. Her palms flew to the door, nails clawing at the wood. Teeth biting into her lower lip, she tried to fight an impending orgasm. When the door handle rattled, a quiver of fear shot through her. That was all it took. An orgasm crashed down over her, swallowing her in its intensity. She convulsed silently, breaths arrested in her throat, mouth open but no noise issuing forth.

The police moved along, and Trini slowly descended from the pinnacle of her orgasm. Simon continued his leisurely licks until she slipped her left knee from his shoulders and awkwardly regained her balance. Squatting down, she slipped an arm around his waist and pulled him close for a kiss. She loved the taste of her cunt on a lover's lips. To her, there was no moment more intimate than the one shared after oral sex.

Later, when Trini remembered their illicit tryst, she couldn't quite recall how they'd ended up on the floor, Simon supine beneath her. His unbuttoned shirt fell away from his body, revealing one hell of a sexy washboard tummy. Trini nipped and licked at his rippled abs and surprisingly sensitive nipples. She unbuckled his belt and lowered the fly on his trousers. The cotton boxers beneath surprised her since she'd always pegged him as a boxer-briefs sort of guy.

As she tugged his trousers and boxers down around his hips, she heard the faintest crinkling noise. Curious, she dug in his left pocket and discovered a condom. Holding it up, she smirked. "Rather presumptuous, aren't we?"

He sat up and tangled his hand in her hair before kissing her. "Just prepared."

Trini laughed and shoved on his shoulders, forcing his back to the carpet. She scooted down his body until her lips were just centimeters from his erect cock. Silver light splashed across their bodies and brought attention to the shimmering drop of precome crowning the head of his penis. Desperate for his taste, she gathered it up with the tip of her tongue. Simon trembled at her initial touch. Power vibrated through Trini.

With a broad swipe, she licked the length of his erection.

She ran her tongue across his tight sac and pulled first his left then his right ball into her mouth. His salty taste and musky scent aroused her. She pooled a bit of saliva on her tongue and allowed it to dribble onto the head of his penis. Licking her palm, Trini slicked her skin before wrapping her fingers around his thick cock and stroking loosely. She took just the top of him into her mouth. Her tongue swirled as she applied suction. Using her hand and mouth, Trini worked Simon into a frenzied state. His hips pumped. His fingers clenched and unclenched. She paid attention to his body language, careful to keep him aroused but never letting him get too close.

"Enough," Simon interrupted, panting with need. "Fuck me. Ride me."

Trini didn't have to be told twice. She frantically patted the carpet for the condom and quickly handed it over once she'd found it. Hands on his chest, Trini balanced over his sheathed erection, her feet planted firmly on the ground. She reached between them to guide his stiff rod into her wet heat and sank down in one breathless move. Both groaned with pleasure.

Not wanting to waste one second of their interlude, Trini immediately bounced up and down on his cock. With each stroke, she bottomed out on him. The little pleasure/pain shock of his dick bumping her womb intensified her excitement. Each strike of her clit against his pelvis rekindled the embers of arousal hidden deep within her. Like a well-oiled piston, she rode him. Simon caressed her body and played with her breasts. He pinched the hardened peaks of her breasts, sending electric shock waves straight to her weeping cunt.

Frantic for more contact, Trini shifted her legs so that her knees rested on either side of his thighs. She bent down and captured his mouth while rocking her pussy and clit back and forth. The crisp hairs covering his chest teased her nipples. He latched on to the sensitive curve of her throat and sucked hard, no doubt intent upon marking her. His possessive act made her even hotter.

When he released her skin with a noisy pop, Trini sat back and rested her hands on his thighs. The change in the angle of penetration was just what she needed. With each movement, his cock slid against her engorged G-spot. She loved that sharply intense sensation. Trini moaned at the feeling of Simon's thumb against her clit. Her pussy clenched as the coil in her belly tightened. Frenzied, she sat up, her hands on her own breasts now, and went wild on Simon's cock. His thumb flicked with increasing speed.

"Come for me, Trini," he gruffly ordered.

And she did. Wave after wave of rapturous pleasure inundated her writhing body. Simon gripped her waist and snapped his hips, pounding his cock into her soaking hole again and again and again. With a strangled growl, he came, jerking once, twice, and then holding perfectly still, his hips still elevated, cock buried inside her.

When he finally relaxed, Trini tumbled off of him and rolled onto her back. No longer lust drunk, she felt the burning ache on her kneecaps. Rug burns, she realized with a wince. Well worth the price of such a torrid affair, she reasoned. She could only imagine how she must have looked at that moment, hair wild, skin flushed. Thoroughly debauched, she supposed.

Out of the corner of her eye, Trini noticed Simon dealing with the aftermath of their copulation. She hoped he'd get rid of it somewhere outside of the president's office. No doubt it would raise eyebrows if a condom was found in the old curmudgeon's trash can.

Simon climbed over Trini, pinning her to the floor with his weight. He stared into her eyes, as if gauging her response to him, to the scorching sex they'd just shared. Starting at the tip of her nose, he kissed his way down her body, pausing at her toes and working his way back up again. He pressed playful kisses up her thighs and around her belly button. She toyed with his hair as he placed his cheek to her tummy and wrapped his arms around her waist. They stayed that way for a while, both enjoying the gentle intimacy of the moment.

Soon, reality struck. Simon helped her stand and they went about the business of righting their clothing. Trini pulled a pair of yoga shorts, a tee, and flip-flops from her backpack and quickly dressed. She grabbed her gloves and mask from the floor and stuffed them into her backpack. She glanced around in search of her G-string but couldn't find it. A movement caught her attention. Simon had his back to her so he didn't see her watching him slip the G-string into his pocket. She shrugged and zipped up her bag. If he wanted a keepsake, she wasn't going to stop him.

They stood awkwardly at the door. Crazy as it sounded, Trini wasn't one to indulge in one-night stands or casual sex. Taking her clothes off for strangers was one thing. Sleeping with them was quite another. Was that what this was? A one-off? Or something else?

"So," Simon said eventually.

"So," Trini repeated uncertainly.

"I suppose I won't see you again until convocation."

Her chest constricted with disappointment. "Probably not."

"And after?"

Trini detected the hopefulness in his voice. She swallowed hard. "After?"

"Maybe you might like to have dinner or something?"

Excitement bubbled in the pit of her tummy. "Dinner sounds nice—and something, too."

Simon grinned, seemingly relieved. "Good. Great." He unlocked the door and poked his head out into the hall. "Coast is clear. Let's go."

They walked down the dark hall, hands and arms bumping. Simon interlaced their hands. Trini marveled at the absolute oddness of this night. She'd expected to go out with a bang but this was just out of this world.

"You know, I fancy a bit of exhibitionism myself."

Trini glanced up at Simon. "That so?"

He nodded. "I've got this bay window at my house that would make the perfect backdrop for a naughty little shadow-puppet show."

Trini's belly clenched with excitement. "Oh really?"

Simon squeezed her hand and waggled his eyebrows. "Consider it a graduation gift."

Trini laughed. "Best graduation gift, like, ever."

Simon chuckled and pecked her cheek. "I've a feeling you and I are going to have one delightfully kinky summer."

"Promise?"

"Promise."

OWNERSHIP

Craig J. Sorensen

Troy opened his eyes and took in the dark ceiling. Syncopated strains of snoring filled the room.

Over the first three weeks of basic training, this room had become home. There was no privacy, there was no spare time except deep in the night. Usually exhausted, he slept right through it. Tonight, the swelling sensation of a hard-on launching up from his tight balls like a rocket was strangely freeing. He hadn't touched or been touched since before he had arrived at Fort Leonard Wood, Missouri. He hadn't even touched his perpetually soft cock except to wash or piss. He'd started to believe the stories about saltpeter being put in the food to keep sexual desires at bay. He stroked the glorious hard-on like it was a magic lamp, and perhaps a genie might grant him a wish.

But, barring this wish, he knew there was no way he could consummate his need in the aptly named "Big Bay," the most populous room situated at the center of the Vietnam-era barracks.

There were so many simple truths in basic training: when he would eat, when he would sleep, what he would learn, how far he would run, how he would walk, what he would wear and when. But the most important truth at this moment was that his chances of getting together with a woman were nil.

He drew his robe from the end of the bed and covered his shoulders like James Brown being walked away from the stage. The latrine was gloriously empty and dark. He slipped into the last stall. He licked his hand and coiled it around his cock then pounded hard and fast for a minute, driving toward a sudden, powerful orgasm. There were dozens of other men sleeping in the barracks who could wake and come into the room anytime. There was no time to waste.

Troy thought of one of those wild nights with his now illus-trious ex-girlfriend Tina. As long as it had been since he'd had an orgasm, it would be so simple to just let the thing loose, splatter all over his stomach and whatever else got in the way. The orgasm began to swell in his hardening balls.

Tina's writing body began to fade.

In the dining room at the Denny's across the parking lot from the Best Western Motel, Troy focused on a nearby table. A willowy blonde sat in a booth across from an attractive brunette with soft feminine curves. The two women talked a blue streak, their hands waving wildly.

Alan followed Troy's eyes, licked his lips and nodded toward the women. "They're in the motel, too, just four doors down."

There was that shared sense of a grand pivot, a change on the wind. Though Alan and Troy had just met that day, they united under a common goal. Tomorrow would be their first day at basic training, sequestered in some Missouri barracks with only their memories and fields of olive drab to keep them company.

The two went back to their motel room and cracked a couple of beers from a twelve-pack of Coors that Troy had bought. A little brewed courage under their belts, they walked down the hall and knocked on the door. There was no answer. They knocked again. "You sure this was the room, Alan?"

"Yeah, yeah, no doubt about it."

"It was a good idea. Let's just have another beer."

"I'm gonna leave a note and invite them down to our room."

"Whatever." Troy returned to their room and stared blankly at the TV. He looked at the phone. "Maybe..."

A sudden splash of cold water awoke Troy. "Fuck!"

"Asshole!" The voice was soft and sweet.

"What the—?"

A pretty brunette with full hips and a soft curved belly in perfectly fitted jeans stood over him with an empty glass. "Love the note, jerk."

"What?" Troy tried to get his bearings.

"The note you left on our door."

"I didn't leave any fucking—" Then Troy remembered.

The brunette looked at her friend who held an equally empty glass pointed toward Alan. Alan grinned at the angry blonde. Water dripped from his chin.

"Uh, that wasn't your note?" The brunette's posture eased.

Troy nodded toward Alan.

She tilted her head and mouthed the word, "Sorry."

Troy wiped his face and hands on the bedspread. "No problem. I'm Troy."

"Kendall."

Kendall's voice fell to a whisper while Alan tried to charm the blonde. "Wanna come down to my room?"

Troy looked down at his wet bed. "Sounds good." He grabbed the rest of the half case of Coors and followed Kendall.

Alan sneered.

"Hey, I fucking bought them," Troy said as he left the room.

Kendall took off her jacket as the two entered her room. The Tarney Spencer Band song "No Time to Lose" squawked out of a cheap radio. She smiled softly.

"Look, I'm really sorry about the note. Alan said he was going to invite you guys down, but it's obvious—"

Kendall waved off the apology. "We're in town to take tests for the Army."

"We're off to basic training in the morning."

"I know."

"How? Oh yeah, the note, right?"

"A request for a nice, you know, night. The last wishes of a condemned man. That sort of thing."

"That stupid fuck."

"You been friends long?"

"Nah, we just met."

"Colleen and I are best friends. We're thinking about joining the Army together."

"Cool." Troy cracked two beers and took a long drink of one to calm his racing heart. There was something enchanting about Kendall.

While Alan had delivered the fabled note, Troy had even tried to call Tina just on the off chance she'd take mercy on him, forget the endless conflicts and remember the great sex. He was glad it hadn't worked as well as Alan's stupid note.

Troy scooted closer to Kendall and handed the other beer to her.

Her eyes were the deep slate color of storm clouds when a small shaft of sunlight had managed to peek through. Her cheeks were bright red with a bit too much blush and her slim lips were slivers of vermilion. Soft blue eye shadow shimmered like mica in a cool riverbed.

Kendall's body language remained shy, but her full hip pressed his. The aroma of mint and beer crossed the tiny divide between their faces. She accepted Troy's first, soft kiss. He moved his lips slowly side to side against hers, and her mouth finally opened a little. His tongue could barely fit in. The tip of her tongue was rough and tasted of malt and honey. She received the kiss awkwardly but a deep moan promised great passion. Troy's cock was hard as a girder. He kissed along her full cheek then gently licked her ear. She moaned, and her soft curves conformed to his skinny frame like a fitted sheath to a balanced blade.

Kendall pushed him gently away and took another drink. He nuzzled her neck until another breathy sigh issued from her chest. Troy unbuttoned the top button of her blouse. Her hand started to rise as if to push him away again, but relaxed and stroked his forearm as he nuzzled again and moved down the blouse. It fell open. Troy pulled off his T-shirt. Kendall combed his chest hairs with her fingers while he untucked her blouse and peeled it from her shoulders. "Umm, just because we took off our shirts—I mean, I don't want you to think we're going to—" Kendall covered her bra with one arm.

"Oh, sure, sure." Troy smiled reassuringly. His cock pushed at his zipper like a lifer on the verge of a prison break. Troy was a skilled fisherman, and knew the essential value of patience.

In the next round of kisses, Kendall slowly lay back on the bed. Troy curled next to her and took off his pants. He did not make any moves toward Kendall's jeans. Finally, she eased out of them, slowly, cautiously. "Just because we took off our pants doesn't mean we're going to—you know," she repeated.

"I know, Kendall."

She turned off the light and slipped into the bed. Troy put the remaining cans of beer on the nightstand and slid between the sheets with her. He massaged her breasts, lingering on large, hard nipples that poked through the satin bra. She moaned into his mouth. His hand drifted down her baby soft skin and came to rest at the top of her panties. He stroked the satin bow at their apex. His fingers slipped under the waistband into the upper reaches of downy pubic hair.

She pressed his chest. "Um, let's just talk."

Troy smiled. "Okay, what do you want to talk about?"

Kendall thought for a moment. "Colleen and I are witches."

"Oh? You don't look like witches."

"What did you expect? Brooms, pointy hats, maybe warts on the nose?"

"Oh I—uh—I dunno."

Kendall took his gaze seriously. "I'm a virgin."

Troy shrugged and forced another smile.

"I don't look like that either?"

He laughed. His body relaxed.

"Disappointed?"

Troy stroked her arm. "Not if you don't plan on staying that way."

Kendall's shrill laugh was bright and beautiful like the green and yellow springtime blouse that glowed in the dim light of the room, sprawled under Troy's faded jeans. "I do, until I'm married."

Troy pushed back the covers and leaned up on one elbow. He took a long drink of his beer and studied Kendall's rounded face in the dark. She was so very pretty.

"It's okay if you want to leave." Kendall tilted her head with sweet understanding.

Troy sighed. "You seem to like the kissing."

Kendall closed her eyes. "Mmm. Yeah, a lot."

He lay back down and pressed his lips to hers again. Her mouth now opened wide. He explored her mouth gently, thoroughly. She leveled her beer upon his back.

"You won't be a virgin for long," Troy said between kisses.

Her hand propped his chest like a forklift. A splash of warm beer streamed along his spine. "What's that mean?" Her eyes blazed in the sparse shards of orange mercury light from the parking lot.

"No, nothing like that. I'm just saying, passionate as you are, I can't see...you lasting long."

"Until I'm married."

"Gotcha."

The two drifted in and out of sleep, serpentine conversation and kisses. At one point, Kendall opened her mouth to speak but was interrupted by a grinding sigh as a key penetrated the lock. "It's Colleen!"

The two lay as if they were sleeping. Kendall yanked the covers modestly over their underwear-clad bodies. She opened one eye and grinned at Troy. "Shh!"

"I think she's asleep, be quiet." It was a feminine whisper. The light from the hall widened into the entryway and two shadowed figures entered the room.

"Awright, awright," a husky male voice whispered back as the door closed.

Kendall's eyes clamped shut. Troy watched across the soft covered terrain of Kendall's body as the couple crept through the dark room. The man squeezed Colleen's butt and she giggled. The two fumbled, their eyes still obviously adjusting from the brightness of the motel hall. "Fuck!" The man bumped his leg into the second queen-sized bed. He and Colleen laughed and she shushed him.

The man wasn't Alan. He was a stocky, large man who was also staying in the motel, and who was readily identifiable by his shiny, cue-ball head.

The couple both looked toward Troy and Kendall. Troy closed his eyes in mock sleep. Whether it fooled the other couple turned out to be a moot point. "Ooh, go Kendall!" Colleen's voice rose up a bit.

Kendall did not even twitch.

Troy waited until he heard moans, then opened his eyes. Colleen and her date were lost in starving python kisses. Amidst their wild groping, Troy leaned up on one arm and reached across Kendall to the nightstand. He finished his half can of beer while the two peeled off their layers of clothes.

Troy popped another beer open without trying to mask the sound. Colleen's head only twisted slightly at the hissing sound. She spread her legs wider and Baldy's thick hand squeezed under the front of her panties.

Troy's cock, which had managed to reach flaccidity before the other couple arrived, grew heavy again.

Colleen's hips curled into Baldy's violent massaging. "Oh god, that's wonderful!" She shoved his boxers down, and his long, thick cock sprung into view.

Troy's hard-on reached full extension, and he pressed to Kendall. He was sure he heard her sigh and felt her hip sway toward him. He looked at her long lashes to see if they might be just a bit open. It was hard to tell. Her breathing was steady, soft and calm. He wanted so badly to be inside Kendall. He kissed her cheek and her impassive face seemed to gently twitch. He kissed her neck. Perhaps her twitch was a gasp. Her heart seemed to be beating hard and fast.

Baldy yanked Colleen's panties down her hips and left them hooked to one ankle as he lifted her hips to his mouth and devoured her pussy. Colleen writhed under the pressure and a hint of a woman's scent colored the room. "Unh. Ohh, gawd yes!" Colleen's voice strained over the little radio, which crackled with The Cars' song "Let the Good Times Roll." She pulled her knees toward her shoulders when Baldy finished eating her and let her hips fall to the bed. He loomed over her lanky body and lowered, forcing her long frame to a tight parcel on the bed. In slow motion his cock slid inside, guided by Colleen's slim fingers, which terminated in long, glossy nails. Her hands roamed desperately up Baldy's powerful arms that suspended him above her chest so his hips could swivel in and out his full length. Colleen's mouth gaped and her head turned slowly toward Troy.

Troy closed his eyes suddenly and listened to Colleen's grunts. He slowly reopened them a sliver. Colleen stared at him. He opened his eyes fully, reached to the nightstand and held up his Coors in a silent toast. Colleen winked, then turned back up toward Baldy, slid her legs along his sides and tangled them in his thighs. Her knees sprawled like yawning scissors with his thrusts.

Troy gulped down the rest of his beer and muffled a belch.

He was sure Kendall smiled. He rested the empty beer on her soft stomach. "Are you asleep?" he whispered in her ear. She didn't make the slightest move, even as the wet, crackling sounds of sex got louder and faster.

Baldy turned over and gave Colleen control. Her long nude body was lined in a dim orange glow, framing thick dark nipples along perky, pale breasts. Her blonde pubic hair gleamed as she pounded on Baldy's hips until his ass jumped a foot off the mattress and suspended Colleen in the air. She bounded with his violent upward thrusts like a rodeo champion on a bucking mustang. Their grunts and groans ascended until Baldy shouted out his orgasm and collapsed like the Tacoma Narrows Bridge to the mattress. Colleen shouted out in reply, and her limbs went limp around Baldy like a crime-scene outline.

Troy lay in the sudden quiet, his cock so hard it ached like a bad tooth.

Baldy and Colleen kissed and fondled and shared quiet jokes.

Troy watched Kendall patiently, awaiting some affirmation of their connection. He reached back under the covers and rested his hand on her stomach. It was so hot it made his chilled fingers tingle like playing barefoot on a cool autumn night, then coming into a warm house. He eased his hand down beneath her belly button. She remained still. He waited for her to express her need. A moan. A sigh. A kiss. A plea, "Please make love to me."

He slid his hand a bit lower until he clasped the little bow of her panties between his thumb and forefinger. She still did not respond. She was still as death.

Baldy and Colleen had since nodded off, their sated nude bodies sprawled exposed on bed.

Troy moved his hand back up to Kendall's stomach, and sensed a deep inhale, an exhale and then steady, soft breaths. He watched her breathe steadily until he nodded off.

"Hey, Troy!"

Kendall tucked her shirt in her jeans. Troy shook the sleep from his head. "When did you say you had to be up to catch your flight?"

"What? Um, seven."

"It's seven now."

"Oh shit!" The next bed was a shambles, covers, sheets scattered. Baldy and Colleen were gone.

Troy gathered his clothes and began to dress.

"And Troy?"

"Hmm?"

Kendall stepped close to him and cupped his chin. She gently rubbed his stubble. "Thanks."

"For what?"

"For not, you know, pushing it. When Colleen and that bald guy were going at it, I mean, then the way your...the way you felt on my hip, and afterward with your hand on me, well, if you had wanted to..."

"Oh god, don't tell me that, Kendall." Troy felt his cock getting heavy again.

Kendall laughed, licked her naked, pink lips and kissed him gently on the cheek. "You're so sweet. Really, thank you."

With only a couple of restless hours of sleep under his belt, Troy nodded off for most of the flight to St. Louis. From the time he'd returned to his room with Alan, he'd had to deflect the other recruit's Spanish Inquisition line of questioning about his night with Kendall.

Finally, he blurted, "Shit Alan, give it rest. Nothing happened, really."

"Yeah, whatever, Troy. Let the good times roll." Alan gave a mocking thumbs-up.

Troy blurted a laugh.

Alan glared at him, unaware of what the song conjured.

Troy was so deep in his memories and the lavish strokes to his cock, that he had not noticed when the light switched on.

"Who shits in the dark?"

Troy froze. The evaporating spit and precome made the tip of his cock grow cold. He sat still as if his silence might make the unwelcome visitor forget he was there. The sound of piss sang in a urinal while a mournful whistle echoed against the tile. "So? Who shits in the dark?"

"Fuck." Troy took the robe from the hook on the back of the stall door and squeezed his hard cock into his briefs. He went to the sink and washed the juices off his hand.

"So, were you jacking off in there?" Alan grinned.

"Why, you wanna watch?"

"Hey, at least you got fucking laid the night before we came here."

"Yeah, whatever, Alan. Let the good times roll." Troy returned to his bed and lay on his stomach. He didn't have anything personal in his wall locker, the small metal box that was his only "private" space now. All was in shades of green and brass and khaki and black, arranged to military-approved perfection.

But he had his hard-on. That was all his, and he pushed his hips down firmly so the soft mattress conformed to it. It felt strangely satisfying. The sight of Kendall's pretty face rimmed in morning light at the Best Western Motel glowed in his memory. He sensed her struggle during that wild night, first from outside himself, like the smell of her strawberry perfume and Secret deodorant that faded against growing sweat, but then from a deeper place. The desperate, steely need in his body, supercharged by the all-sense images of Baldy and Colleen fucking wildly in the next bed, bodies exposed in exhibitionistic glory, connected him with Kendall. He united with her hard-fought restraint.

He'd never answered Kendall when she'd thanked him. "You're welcome, Virgin Witch. I'm truly glad I didn't push it."

"What?"

Troy looked up to see Alan stopped midstride as he passed by in the dark barracks room. "Let the good times roll." Troy held a thumbs-up.

"Go fuck yourself, Troy."

Kendall would still be there, bewitching his memory, when he got out of basic training in three more weeks. Somehow, he figured he could wait. "Thanks, Alan. Maybe later."

AUDIENCE PARTICIPATION

Elizabeth Coldwell

The webcam was Tony's brainchild; I think he viewed it as some big, sociological experiment that would bring the work of our department to a wider world. The rest of us thought it was just a big waste of time.

He came up with the idea after reading an article in a magazine supplement about the webcam phenomenon; how the concept had been commercialized—as had just about every aspect of the Internet—by the pornographers, who charged subscribers through the nose to watch the feed from what was supposedly a suburban bedroom, where girls wandered around in their underwear, occasionally using sex toys and their own fingers on themselves or some willing friend. However, what really interested Tony were the quirky little projects that were not intended for financial gain: the camera trained on a coffee pot bubbling in some corner of a California university campus; the view of a British medical library that had gained cult status among Australian students, who would log on to look at it in the middle of the night, darkened and deserted. Tony seemed to believe that a webcam focusing on our own research and development department would attract a similar following, and though none of us shared his enthusiasm for the project, we were happy to let him get on with it, if only because it would distract him from breathing down our necks every minute of the working day.

The irony was that our own access to the Internet was so restricted, we would probably never get the chance to watch ourselves going about our daily tasks. Tony believed that if we had it installed on our computers, we would spend all day wasting time on it. The IT department had already ensured that no one could access any site that promoted gambling, had chatroom facilities or offered the opportunity to ogle naked, busty Scandinavians. But that wasn't enough for Tony; he was convinced that we would use it to book cheap flights when we should be working—never mind that on our wages we barely had the spare cash for a day trip to Brighton—or that Gary would be poking girls on Facebook all day. So the only terminal in the department that had Internet access was Tony's, and if we needed to look anything up in the course of our research, we practically had to get down on our knees and beg him to let us use it.

Still, if Tony was the only person involved with the setting up of the webcam project, it would mean minimal contact for the rest of us with the IT staff. In the two years I had been working for the department, I had dreaded any problem developing on my PC that needed a visit from whichever techie was assigned to fix it. It was difficult to know who had been the least pleasant to deal with: Miles, who went Morris-dancing at weekends and was obsessed with "Buffy the Vampire Slayer"; Dean, the Essex wide boy who treated me as if I was eight years old and barely to be trusted with a sharp pencil, let alone a grand's worth of computer equipment; or Kieran, the uncooperative South African, who

would finally deign to amble down from the fourth floor and
sort out the fault two days after it had been reported. I would
rather return to writing up my findings in longhand with a ball-
point pen and working my calculations out on my fingers than
have IT fix anything else for me. Until I saw Chris.

Actually, it was his arse I saw first. Well, I could hardly miss
it, seeing as it was facing me across the workbench, covered in
very faded denim that stretched tautly over two perfect, firm
cheeks. There was no one else in the room and I moved closer,
fighting the instinct to reach out a hand and stroke this beautiful bum. My foot knocked against a metal wastepaper bin and
the sound caused him to spin round, startled. The front view
was as enticing as the rear: blue eyes peered out from beneath
a bleached-blond fringe, and his boyish features broadened in a
smile as he looked at me.

"I'm just checking you've got enough sockets for us to install
the camera equipment," he explained, raising himself to his full
height. This was getting better by the second. He must have been
all of six foot two, and worth the climb. "I'm Chris, by the way."

"Kat Parker," I replied. "Go on, make my day. Tell me it's
not going to be possible."

"Sorry, everything looks to be in order. Why, aren't you
looking forward to your moment of fame?"

I laughed. "You make it seem like I'm about to check into
the 'Big Brother' house. No, I just don't want to be part of my
boss's ego trip. I mean, if he wanted to get involved in a serious
scientific side project, he could keep an eye on whatever it is
that's growing in the dirty coffee cup that's been on Gary's desk
for a fortnight."

"Don't be so dismissive, Kat," Chris said. "Sometimes it's
good to be open to new experiences."

I felt like telling him I'd been thinking of a few of those ever since I'd clapped eyes on his denim-clad backside, but at that moment Gary wandered in, balancing a pile of manila folders on top of which rested a grease-spotted brown paper bag, containing his regulation breakfast of an egg and bacon muffin.

"Put the kettle on, Kat, I'm parched," he said, barely glancing in my direction as he let the folders slither from his grasp onto the desk.

Chris glanced at his watch. "I'd better get back upstairs and find out if anyone's howling for me. I'll see you later." And he gave me a cheeky little wink that sent a pang of lust arrowing straight down to my groin.

In the end, I must have seen Chris another half a dozen times throughout the course of the day, as he wandered in and out of the lab with some piece of equipment or other, or used one of the phones to ring the IT department and get instructions on what to do next. I would catch his eye as I reached into the fume cupboard or looked up from the notes I was scrawling on a foolscap pad and he would smile at me. I would fight the irresistible mental image I had of brushing all my work off the bench, hauling him onto the smooth wooden surface and climbing on top of him to fuck his brains out.

Normally, Tony would have spotted the dreamy expression on my face and the complete lack of attention I was paying to the flask of chemicals boiling away unattended over the Bunsen burner and hauled me into his office for a not-so-quiet word. Tony didn't approve of anything less than 100 percent concentration on my work. Mind you, he didn't approve of quite a few of the things I did, from having a burgundy streak in my long, fair hair to wearing miniskirts and tiny tops beneath my lab coat to listening to stoner rock on headphones when I was typing up my notes. It didn't fit in with his image of a department full of sober scientists, dedicated to the pursuit of knowledge. Today, though, I could have probably got up and performed a naked lap dance on his desk without him being aware of it. He seemed even more mesmerized by Chris than I was, hovering at his shoulder as he installed the various component parts of the webcam.

"When will it be working?" I heard Tony asking him toward the end of the afternoon. "When can I get a demonstration?"

"Should be up and running tomorrow morning," Chris answered blithely. "Don't worry, Dr. Wilkins, you'll be broadcasting to the world soon enough."

With that, Chris disappeared back up to the IT department, and I thought I'd seen all I was going to see of him for the day. So I was a little surprised when, last out of the lab as I often had been over the previous couple of weeks, I found him standing in the lobby. His face brightened as I walked toward him, and I realized he'd been waiting for me.

"I was starting to think I must have missed you," he said. "I mean, your boss came through here ages ago. I was thinking maybe you'd rappelled out of the window."

I laughed. "In this skirt? Hardly. No, Tony said he had to be off bang on time tonight, had a dentist's appointment, I think he said, so I told him I'd finish up a couple of things before I left."

"Well, what I wanted to ask you is, are you doing anything tonight?"

"I hadn't made any plans." It was only partly a lie. I hadn't got an evening with the girls lined up, but I had been intending to go home and have a long, foamy, candlelit bath, accompanied by a glass of wine, while my fingers strayed beneath the waterline to stroke my pussy as I built on my fantasy of fucking Chris over the desk.

"Well, do you fancy coming round to mine for something to eat and a demonstration of the webcam?"

"But I thought you told Tony—"

"—That it'll be ready tomorrow? Yeah, but we got all the software installed quicker than we thought we would, and it's actually up and operating now. I reckoned I'd give it a dummy run, check for any glitches in the system before I show your boss the setup in the morning."

It was more of an explanation than I'd needed. I'd have gone round and stared at that screen saver with the flying toasters for a couple of hours if it had meant spending that time in Chris's company. "Okay, then," I said, "your place it is."

Chris lived in a large, second-floor flat in a converted Victorian house ten minutes' walk across the park from where the department was based. It wasn't exactly the grotty rented bedsit I'd been expecting him to live in, particularly as I'd discovered on the way there that he was still only twenty-one, and this was his first job after leaving university. As I wandered into the spacious, sparklingly clean kitchen, which wouldn't have looked out of place in the pages of an interior design magazine, I couldn't help murmuring, "Working in IT must pay a hell of a lot better than I thought."

"Oh, this is my brother's flat," Chris explained, seeing the look of surprise mixed with envy on my face. "I'm house-sitting while he and his missus are on a round-the-world trip. They were learning to scuba dive off the Barrier Reef, the last time I had an email from him." He smiled that crotch-melting smile again. "Until this morning, I almost wished I was with them."

We'd stopped on the way to the flat to buy kung pao chicken and special fried rice from a nearby Chinese takeaway. We opened a bottle of sauvignon blanc and sat in the living room, chill-out music playing softly on the expensive sound system as we ate, but in truth I did little more than rearrange the food on my plate. Chris had chosen to perch alongside me on the two-seater gray leather sofa, and I could feel the taut length of his thigh resting against my own. A pulse was beating between my legs, slow and insistent, and I wanted to press Chris's fingers there, let him feel the effect he was having on me.

When he suddenly pushed his plate away and said, "Come into the bedroom," I thought for a moment he'd read my mind. Then he added, "It's where the PC is. Bring the rest of the wine, I'll boot the system up and we can see if the webcam's working."

I almost told him to stuff the webcam, but then I reminded myself that, nice arse or not, at heart he was still a techie, and they all probably classed switching on a computer as foreplay. So I topped up our glasses and obediently followed him into the bedroom.

The PC was glowing in a corner, going through its routine of warming up and welcoming Chris to the Day-Glo world of Windows. I sat on the big double bed, sipping my drink and wondering whether he'd notice if I hiked up my skirt and started playing with myself.

A few clicks of the mouse and he was logged on to the Internet and typing in the address that would link him to the webcam.

"This may seem like a silly question," I said, "but even if this thing is working, will we actually see anything? I mean, there won't be any lights on in the lab."

Except the ones nearest the door were. Chris beckoned me over to look at the small box in the corner of the screen that was successfully showing the webcam feed, and I realized I was seeing the view from the front of the room, looking out in the direction of Tony's corner office. How typical of him to have ensured his comings and goings would be the center of attention, I thought. I assumed the cleaner must have left the lights on, since I knew I had turned them all off myself before leaving the lab, but just as I was about to congratulate Chris on his technical achievement and persuade him to turn that thing off and let me turn him on, I noticed two shadowy figures coming into view.

"Can you increase the size of the picture?" I asked.

"Sure," Chris replied, and within seconds the image was filling most of the screen. I had expected the pictures to be jerky and slow-moving, lagging behind real time, but Chris—or, more accurately, his brother—obviously had a broadband connection, and while the quality was a little grainy, we could both tell immediately that one of the people we were looking at was Tony.

"Who's the woman with him?" Chris asked. "If that's his dentist, I wouldn't mind her having a poke around in my cavities."

She was taller than my boss, with dark hair caught in a clip at the nape of her neck. I stared at her for a couple of moments before placing her. "No, she works for us, in Human Resources. I think she's called Denise something-or-other. But what are they doing there at this time of—?"

I broke off as my question became redundant. Tony had pressed his companion up against the wall and was kissing her while he tugged her sweater out of her skirt.

"They're not," I said, unable to mesh my knowledge of my straight-laced, work-obsessed—and, most importantly, very married—boss with what I was seeing. "They can't be!"

"Looks to me like they are," Chris replied. He was behind me now, staring at the PC over my shoulder, and his body was tight against mine, a hard, unmistakable lump in his jeans digging into the cheek of my bum.

We shouldn't be looking at this, I told myself, not if things were going to go as far as I suspected. Indeed, my hand actually snaked out toward the mouse, ready to break the Internet connection. And then I stopped, weighing the morality of the situation. Which was worse—having sneaky sex with someone who definitely wasn't your wife, or secretly watching that sex take place? From the rapt expression on Chris's face, reflected in the computer monitor, I knew he was equally intrigued by what was about to happen.

On-screen, Denise's sweater had come off. She had big breasts, confined in a plain white bra, and Tony had his head between them and was nuzzling into her cleavage. My own nipples tingled and pressed against the fabric of my thin cotton top, suddenly aching for the same treatment hers were clearly getting. Almost unconsciously, I pushed my rump back against Chris's groin, grinding myself against his erection. Ready to reach round and clamp his hands to my tits myself if he didn't take the hint, I sighed as I felt him take hold of me round the waist before his fingers began to stray that little bit higher. Slowly, slowly they moved until they were brushing my nipples. I caught my breath, daring him to go farther.

Tony, I noticed, had pulled Denise's breasts out of the cups of her bra, and had his mouth latched greedily on to one hard nipple while his fingers squeezed the other. There was no audio feed from the webcam, but from the way the woman's head was thrown back, mouth wide open, it was clear she must be moaning her pleasure at what he was doing to her.

My pussy was pulsing more urgently than ever, demanding attention. I couldn't believe how horny I was getting just looking at the couple in the lab. I'd never even considered the idea that I might possess a voyeuristic streak until this moment. An ex-boyfriend and I had once watched a porn video that had been doing the rounds among the lads on the shop floor where he worked, but though he'd sat through the film with his hand clamped to his swollen erection, it had done nothing for me;

I just didn't find the big, obviously fake tits and the ridiculous "Ooh, baby, fuck my pussy" dialogue at all sexy. But this was different: this was real, two people sharing what they thought was a moment of private lust, not knowing that, in another part of town, a couple of pairs of greedy eyes were taking in everything they were doing.

Taking it in, and getting really excited by it. Chris's voice had noticeably thickened as he muttered, "A mate I was at university with had a summer job looking after the CCTV in a multistory car park. He told me he used to see this sort of thing on a Friday night after the pubs had cleared out, but I always thought he was winding me up."

"Well, it's amazing what people will get up to when they think nobody's watching them," I replied.

"Like this, you mean?" I felt Chris fumbling with the halter fastening of my top; he pulled it apart and the fabric flopped down to my waist, baring my breasts to his touch. His hands were so big they covered the firm little mounds completely, my nipples peeking out cheekily between his fingers. I tried to reach back for his zip, anxious to feel his cock in my hand and find out if it was as solidly built as the rest of him, but he caught hold of my wrist, then brought my other arm round to join it, pinning both briefly in his grasp. I had been so busy trying to force the pace, it had never occurred to me until this moment that he might have a thing about being in control. I had visions of him binding my wrists together with his belt, restraining me properly before he fucked me, and the thought almost had me moaning out loud. "Don't be greedy, Kat," he whispered. "All in good time."

I felt Chris's hand gently easing its way under the hem of my skirt, and that was when he discovered my naughty little secret.

"Fucking hell, you haven't got any knickers on," he breathed.

"Well, it gets so hot in that place at times, I like to wear as little as possible," I told him. "I'd go completely bare under my lab coat, if I thought I could get away with it."

"God, if I'd known about this at work, I'd never have got the job finished," Chris groaned, his fingers exploring the contours of my exposed sex. "I'd have been hard all day, just thinking about you like this, all wet and available."

His thumb settled on my clit, and began to rub it in a slow, steady rhythm with just enough pressure to send all the nerve endings in my body screaming for more. My eyes flicked back to the action on the monitor, as if I was hypnotized. Tony had slithered his way down Denise's body, and she was holding her skirt up to her waist as his head bobbed up and down at the apex of her thighs. I wanted a better view, the luxury of a close-up, as he licked her. I could imagine exactly what he was doing to her, how his tongue was burrowing into all her folds and crevices, but I wanted to see it for myself.

Behind me, I heard the rasp of Chris's zip coming down. For a moment I was disappointed; I had been hoping that he would follow Tony's example and go down on me. But he obviously wanted to keep watching what Denise and Tony were doing as much as I did, and he couldn't do that if his head was buried between my legs.

I felt the head of his cock nudging at the entrance to my cunt, eager to find its way inside. I parted my legs a little more, opening myself for him. As he slid into me, I groaned. He was big, and it had been longer than I cared to admit since I had last enjoyed a good fuck. Despite that, I still wanted as much of him as he could give me.

Glancing back to see what the couple on-screen were doing, I could hardly believe my eyes. Demonstrating an athleticism I would never have expected him to possess in a million years, my boss had hoisted his lover up so she could wrap her legs around his waist and he was fucking her against the wall, standing up. I tried to concentrate on the action in front of me, but it was becoming increasingly difficult, given the way Chris was thrusting into me. I was stretched tightly around the thickness of his shaft, every thrust stimulating places that had forgotten what it was like to be touched. Chris was murmuring in my ear how tight I was, and how good it felt, and I just gave myself up to the waves of sensation that were rolling through me and came, hard, as Tony and Denise slumped against the wall, obviously spent. I heard Chris give a deep groan, and then he, too, was coming, holding me tightly as his body jerked against mine.

"Thank you, Kat," he said when he was able to speak again, his lips brushing my neck in the lightest of kisses.

"No, thank you," I replied. "This webcam of yours has really opened my eyes to the wonders of modern technology."

He laughed. "Not to mention your legs." We looked back to the screen, but the lab was now in darkness and Tony and Denise had gone, presumably still thinking their secret was safe. "You enjoyed that, didn't you?"

"More than I ever thought I would," I admitted.

"Well, I tell you what," Chris said, spinning me round to face him and clasping my wrists together in the gesture that suggested, given time, he would be thoroughly exploring the kinky side he now knew I possessed, "now you know what it's like to do the watching, why don't we give it a couple of days, wait till the site's in a few search engines and people start logging on, and then we can go down to the lab and find out what it's like to be watched...."

NOW YOU SEE HER

Andrea Dale

So, what do you think of Emilie's latest?" Shane asked.

I laughed, thinking of our friend's new assistant, whom we'd just met tonight: pretty, but not sure what to do with it; eyes wide and dazzled by the whirlwind force that is Emilie, not to mention by the city, the club, the people.

"I think she doesn't quite know what she's in for," I said. My gloved fingers were already laced with Shane's as we walked the final few blocks from the metro to our apartment, and I swung our arms back and forth, because I felt giddy and also to keep myself warm. The night sky was clear, although Montréal's lights kept the stars dimmed. It hadn't snowed—yet.

I hoped it would soon. At least that would take the edge off the bitter cold.

"What do you mean?" Shane asked.

"Oh, you know Emilie," I said.

"No, I don't, not really." He tilted his head in that curious way that made my heart stutter. "Tell me."

Of course. Silly me. He was friends with Emilie because she and I had been roommates in college and remained close since—but he didn't know her like I did.

"I'll tell you when we get home!" I said, and we took off running, as best we could, anyway, with me in killer heels.

Inside, his wire-rimmed glasses fogged as we shivered and shucked our coats and scarves and hats. I put on water for tea, curled next to him on the sofa under the framed black-and-white prints of Old Quebec he'd taken. I tucked my cold feet under me for warmth.

"Tell me about Emilie," he urged.

"Katy, her new assistant?" I said. "Emilie tends to take girls like that under her wing. That's who she's attracted to: the kind who are a little naïve but eager to learn. And I don't just mean about running an art gallery or how to dress well and do their hair."

"Sex," Shane said. His breath, warm against my neck, made me shiver, and not from a chill, either.

I was still tipsy from the appletinis I'd had at the club. "Emilie can be...a little kinky," I admitted.

He'd rested his head on mine, and I felt him smile. "Was she with you?"

In the interest of openness and honesty in a relationship, I'd told him how Emilie and I had had a fling in college. It was my year of experimentation, and in the end I'd happily decided I wasn't all that interested in girls. Pretty and sexy to look at, but playing with them wasn't a big deal for me. Emilie hadn't taken offense, and our friendship stayed just as strong as it had been.

"No," I said. "I decided girls weren't my thing before we got to that level. But I had a front-row seat to watch her with her other girlfriends."

The kettle whistled, and I got up to make the tea. When I got back with the two steaming mugs, Shane had divested himself of his pants. His boxers were tented, and he loosely caressed his cock through the silk.

"Well," I said, carefully putting the steaming mugs out of harm's way, "aren't we the aural voyeur."

"I like it when you tell me stories," he said with that cheeky grin of his.

"I'm not saying I sat up and watched Emilie and her conveyer belt of girls," I said. "But I saw some of it firsthand—I couldn't not, really, since that's part of Emilie's kink. And we talked about it." I couldn't help smiling at the memories. Emilie's openness had helped me come out of my own sexual shell.

"She's dominant, but not in a major whips-and-chains kind of way," I went on. "She's into spanking a little, but more for the effect than the pain. She likes to push people, likes to find their limits and see if she can squeak them past the lines they think they've drawn."

Shane slipped the straps of my chemise down, drew circles around my beading nipples, teasing, arousing. I squirmed.

"Her main thing is exhibitionism. She likes to show off, likes to show off her partners. Likes to humiliate them a little bit, but not in a mean way." I was having trouble thinking, between the aftereffects of the martinis and Shane's skillful hands making my blood rush from my brain to pool in my groin. "Am I making any sense?"

"Oh, yes," he said. "You definitely are. Keep talking."

"Don't want to," I said, reaching for him.

He braceleted my wrist with his fingers, pulled me away. "Yes," he said. "You're enjoying this just as much as I am."

I sighed, tried to focus through the haze of pleasure. "She likes to have sex in front of mirrors, to have her girlfriends watch themselves as they come. Or in a semipublic place, where someone might see. In front of a window. Nothing turns her on more than knowing her girlfriend is walking next to her in a short skirt and no panties when it's breezy. She won't let them reach down to catch the skirt when it fluffs up...

"I guess what really turns her on is how the girlfriend will blush, but also get so wet. If the anticipation, the possibility of being seen, gets the girlfriend hot, that's what does it for Emilie."

I said it all in a rush, as fast as I could, because I wanted out of my clothes, wanted Shane out of his, wanted to dive onto his cock—which was causing a dark spot of moisture on the silk. I peeled off my herringbone tights, and he didn't protest.

"She wants to bring out the exhibitionist tendencies they don't know they have," Shane summarized.

"Even as they still think they don't have them—she gets off on the power to make them do something they think they didn't want to do even as *they* get off on it."

"Devious." Shane's voice held admiration. "And a nice treat for voyeurs everywhere."

"Mm," I agreed, in part because he'd slipped a hand beneath my skirt and was stroking my clit; lightly, through my panties, not enough to get me off but enough to ratchet me to a new level of need.

I caught a whiff of my own spicy scent, knew I was staining my underwear, too.

"Like I said, I had a front-row seat for most of it." It was clear that if I kept talking, Shane would continue to reward me. Fun! "Even though I didn't want to join in, it was hot to watch. I'd get myself off watching her slide a dildo into her latest conquest, whispering that the girl mustn't make any noise and wake her roommate, even though Emilie knew damn well I was awake and watching. The girl would bite her lip, bury her face in the pillow, whimper... Emilie was good, though, and could always make her cry out in the end."

Then I stopped talking and caught my breath, because Shane whipped aside my panties and, finding me as wet as I suspected I was, slipped two fingers easily into me while his thumb found my exposed clit.

And then I was crying out, helplessly bucking against his hand and coming deliciously hard.

Speaking of deliciously hard, when I was able to see past the stars again, Shane was naked and his cock was within my grasp. I pushed him back on the sofa and straddled him.

Seems he found Emilie quite inspiring, too.

The idea formed in my brain that night, but I didn't have the wherewithal to fully conceive it until later. (We were rather busy, shall we say.)

"Early Christmas present," I said when Shane wondered aloud why we were getting a swish room in a posh hotel halfway across the city, halfway through December. "Prices are crazy closer to the holiday, but they have good deals now." It wasn't a lie—they really did. Even if I *had* paid a little extra to ensure I got a room on the floor I wanted, facing the direction I wanted.

It had snowed earlier that evening, making Montréal look a little like a fairyland. I flung open the curtains. The plate-glass windows looked out onto that magic...and across to something else.

Shane was even more confused—and intrigued—when he realized I'd packed his photography equipment. We'd been together long enough that I knew what he'd need.

"Set it up," I said, "with the tripod. I'll be right back."

I fluffed out my hair, touched up the gloss on my lips, and shimmied into a formfitting lace-and-sheer-mesh baby doll with attached garters: burgundy, setting off my blonde hair.

Yeah. Two steps out of the bathroom and Shane was all over me, hands and mouth, murmuring his approval. It took a great effort on my part to push him away long enough to say "Wait. There's more."

He assumed the photo shoot would be of me (not that we hadn't done that before). I pointed out the window and explained.

"I had a little chat with Emilie," I said, and felt a jolt of pure arousal at the way Shane's green eyes widened with excitement. "She promised us a show tonight; said it would be delightful if we caught it on film." I gestured out the window. "Didn't you realize that's her condo over there?"

"Not until now," Shane said, and captured my mouth in a searing, toe-curling kiss that promised so much sexy goodness to come.

He repositioned the tripod and I raised the binoculars just in time to see the curtains across the way twitch open. Emilie stood there, naked, and I knew she didn't care if anyone was watching.

Then I saw her glance our way, and wink. We were too far away for her to see us, but she knew we were there.

Oh, Katy. You have no idea what you've gotten yourself into.

Emilie settled onto a hassock and leaned back, her lithe body arching languorously as she parted her legs. Shane muttered "Oh, *yeah*," and I almost laughed. The sound caught in my throat as Katy, responding to Emilie's beckoning, sank to her knees in front of the other woman. Katy's face was hidden by Emilie's thigh, but her body was highlighted in glorious profile.

We watched, via zoom lens and binoculars, as Katy brought Emilie to orgasm. Emilie wasn't posing when she came; that much I knew. Her writhing was abandoned.

I slipped my fingers between my legs, coated them in my juices, and brought them to Shane's mouth.

"Does Katy know we're here?" he asked hoarsely as he stripped down to his boxers.

"I don't think so," I said. "I think Emilie's telling her anybody could be watching."

"Makes it more dangerous," he said.

I knelt and breathed hot breath on his burgeoning cock, which twitched beneath the silk. "Mm, doesn't it?" I said.

As much as I wanted to stay and play, I wanted to watch the show even more. I stood and brought up the binoculars again.

Emilie had Katy on her lap. As she teased Katy's nipples, Katy ground herself against Emilie's thigh. She was probably forgetting about the open curtains....

But then Emilie pulled her up and gave her a little push toward the floor-to-ceiling windows.

She really was lovely, pale with dark hair, big dark eyes, lush red lips. She had smallish breasts, but her nipples were huge. She still had a hesitant walk, but maybe that was because she wasn't sure what Emilie was going to ask her to do.

I had to shift my own position because I was fogging up our window. As I did, my thong rubbed against my clit, reminding me—as if I didn't already know—how aroused I was.

Shane was taking picture after picture, glancing up from the camera every so often to just watch the action across the street. Emilie was spanking Katy, and while Katy's hips jerked forward every time Emilie's palm landed, they rolled in pleasure in between the blows. I doubted Katy was even aware she was doing it, and I wished we had a video camera as well.

Now Katy had her hand between her thighs, and I gave up trying to keep the binoculars perfectly steady because I had to do the same thing with *my* hand.

I jumped when Shane caressed my ass.

"I don't know where to look," he confessed.

I kissed him, tasting myself on him. "Watch our show," I said. "You can see me later."

But when Emilie stalked back into view, a harness around her hips sporting a fiendish dildo, Shane gave up trying to take pictures. He slid down my thong; I kicked it away. As Emilie slid into Katy, Shane slid into me.

I dropped the binoculars. I could still see that Katy's breasts were mashed against the window, that her mouth was open.

We had the lights off, of course, but I didn't care if anybody could see us. All I cared about was the feeling of Shane's thick cock inside me, his hands gripping hard on my hips as he thrust faster and faster.

Sweet pleasure built in my groin, harder and hotter. I reached down, grazed my nails along Shane where I could reach him, then flicked my finger across my clit. I was on my second orgasm when he growled and came with me.

Panting, I rested my cheek against the cold glass. I couldn't see through the condensation, but I hoped Emilie and Katy were having just as good a time as we were.

For Christmas, we sent a portfolio of the best shots to Emilie. She promised to give us a full report of how Katy reacted to them.

Or, she said with a wicked smile, she might just make Katy tell us herself.

WATCHER IN THE SHADOWS

Cheyenne Blue

He had the smallest dressing room again. Three bulbs had burned out above the mirror, which was so old that the reflection had worn thin in places, giving his complexion a blotchy, tired appearance. The janitor had left his mop and bucket in the corner, along with a pile of chemicals that would probably remove the spirit gum that held his day-old stubble in place far better than the stuff he used. Someone had divided the room with a sagging curtain, a cursory attempt to hide a pile of broken folding chairs and maintain the illusion that this was a performer's space. But Billy thought himself lucky to have a room at all—so many drag kings were given odd spaces; not quite rooms, not quite hallway corners.

His was the opening act, the one that came on while the audience was still shuffling through the foyer, or jawing in the bar, swilling cheap wine from plastic cups. His act was always interrupted by loud curses as people stubbed their toes finding their seats in the dark, and the dull undertow of a hundred conversations that were too important to wait, especially not for him, King Billy, who was only on the tour because the arts funding needed a nonmainstream act as its nod to diversity. This evening had been no different.

Billy threw himself down in the chair in front of the mirror and systematically began removing the heavy theatrical makeup. Audience laughter filtered down to him, here in his under-stage cell, the appreciative roar and foot-stomping applause that is balm to a performer's soul. His hand reached for the bottle and he poured himself a finger of whiskey, downed it in one gulp.

He was stretching for the bottle again when he heard the sound: a breath, heavy in the sudden audience silence, the sound of someone carefully changing position.

"Who's there?" he barked, but if there was an answer, it was drowned out by the audience noise, once again filtering down through the boards above.

Only silence greeted him. Billy was pouring more whiskey when he heard the definite sound of a foot dragging across the floor. The sound came from behind the curtain. Pushing aside the bottle, Billy stalked across the room. Some kid, no doubt, spying on him, trying to see what was underneath the costume.

"Please don't."

He paused, unsure if he'd imagined the words.

"Please don't pull back the curtain."

He waited, one hand on the dusty cloth. "So, I should let you spy on me?"

"I'm not spying. Not exactly. I just don't want you to see me." The voice was low, the gender blurred by the husky words.

"That's spying in my book."

The pause stretched. Billy imagined his unseen watcher in the shadows; mortified maybe, embarrassed at having been caught. But when the intruder spoke again, the voice was challenging.

"So, say something. Do you like the idea of being watched? Do you like the thought of me watching your body, watching you take your clothes off? Peering to see if—"

"Enough." Billy yanked hard on the curtain, and a cloud of dust and hairs billowed out. "Tell my why I shouldn't call security?"

"But you haven't. How long now? Five minutes? Ten? You're still here, falling into your whiskey with your makeup smeared across your face and I'm still here, watching you."

"Maybe I've had enough. Maybe I want to get changed, go and find a bar somewhere to forget about this evening. Maybe I want to go home and have a wank."

Laughter spluttered out. "Now that I'd like to see."

"You think I don't? Or you wonder how I do it?"

"I'm sure you do it. Doesn't everyone? I'm sure you're no different."

"Even you?"

"No. I don't really exist. I'm just a voice behind the curtain."

"If I pull it back, I can disprove that. What are you doing behind there? Are you too scared to come out, or are you getting some thrill out of this?" With casual deliberation, Billy returned to the mirror, and the heavy makeup came away with long swipes of the sponge. His own face stared back at him, his skin dull and pockmarked, the harsh lighting adding years to his age.

"Why, I'm looking at you of course. Didn't we already establish that?"

"I'm not very exciting. The audience tonight already proved that."

"A general audience who is here to see someone else. I'm here to see you. I find you extremely exciting."

Female. The watcher in the shadows was definitely female.

That last husky catch in her voice had given her away. A female watching him...now that was different; that was exciting. That had possibilities.

Billy ran a hand through his hair, pushed back the forelock that flopped over his eyes and watched the curtain in the mirror. "What would you like to see?"

"What are my options?"

"See the monkey dance. See the monkey scratch himself. See the monkey—"

"Take off his clothes?"

He paused, searching the stranger's words for any hint of laughter, a trickle of condescension, but found neither. No, her voice was steady, as if these were the words she'd been waiting to say. His hand had moved to the top button of his damp shirt before the spurt of anger rose again.

"Why? Want to see what I look like underneath? Want to check out my bindings and my bulges? Get your kicks some other way, lady." He spat the word with disdain and a gob of spittle landed on his shirt.

In the ensuing silence, Billy poured another finger of whiskey and downed it in one swallow. It burned fiery, nearly as hot as the anger simmering hot and urgent in his throat.

When she spoke again, her voice was steady. "Do you normally question the motives of people who want to see you naked? Is it too hard to believe that I think you're hot?"

"Hot?" The whiskey glass shattered against the door, and Billy took a draught from the bottle. "The women who think I'm hot have the guts to prove it. They don't hide behind the curtains like their mama's skirts. They show themselves and let me see the heat in their eyes; they kiss me, grope me, and I feel them back, feel their breasts, and grind my cock against their curvy asses. They let me take down their panties and push my fingers deep in their cunts. Let me eat them, and taste them, and then fuck them until we both come."

"Show me." These low words were spoken with a commanding intensity. When Billy hesitated, unsure as to her meaning, she hissed again, "I said, show me."

"Show you what?"

"Show me what you do."

He laughed. "You'll have to show yourself first."

"Not yet. Now, take off your shirt."

Billy's hands went to the top button. Maybe it was the whiskey, or maybe it was the smoky low quality of his watcher's voice, but he stood, slipped the buttons and shrugged out of his shirt. He caught a glimpse of himself in the mirror. The flesh-colored bandages were hardly aesthetic, but they did the job. Sucking in his stomach, he turned to face the curtain.

"Good abs. You don't need to pose. Now sit down on that chair."

The voice was growing in confidence, choreographing his movements, his disrobing, and even, he realized with a thrill, his desire. His nipples throbbed against the constricting binding, and the warmth slipped down into his belly, where it coiled, lambent and throbbing like a living thing. He pulled the chair away from the dresser into the middle of the room and sat, moving to cup his cock.

"Not until I say!" The voice cracked like ice cubes in gin.

Above them, the stomping of feet and more applause told him that the audience was moving out for the intermission. Billy's hands moved up, tracing his own lips. Closing his eyes, he tried to put a face to the voice. A brunette, he decided, copper hair, dark like mahogany; big breasts, plump and soft like bags of flour, sweet scented, smelling of baby powder. His own nipples pressed painfully against the constriction.

"Now, kiss yourself," the voice ordered.

He stared. "Kiss myself where?"

A tsk of impatience followed. "Didn't you ever kiss your fist when you were a kid, pretending you were French-kissing your pinup girl? Do that...and pretend it's me."

"You could come out here, and I wouldn't have to pretend!"

"I said, do it."

He raised his clenched fist to his lips, leaving a small gap between thumb and first finger. Embarrassment warred with arousal—what sort of idiot idea was this?—but his pride rose. He was a performer, damn it. He'd show her what she was missing, crouched like a frightened bird among the stacked chairs. His tongue flickered lightly against his fist, running over the finger, before insinuating itself into the gap. The heat of his breath rebounded moistly onto his face. Closing his eyes, he substituted soft female lips and smoky bourbon-sweet breath for his fist. Widening the gap, he pushed his tongue farther in, as if this were a real kiss.

Would she kiss like this? he wondered. Would she open her lips for him, press her breasts against his chest and grind herself on his cock? The image made him gasp; his eyes opened and he lowered his fist, abruptly feeling foolish.

The harsh lighting made him wince, and the tiny room was filled with the sounds of shuffling feet and muted chatter—the audience returning from the bar after the interval.

"Did I taste good? Sweet and young?"

"Yeah," he muttered, and the image of her, crouched in the dark, slender arms wrapped around her knees, her eyes burning holes in the curtain, seared his eyeballs.

"Now undo your pants."

"Why?"

A sigh. "Just do it."

Billy complied, and let the dark pants gape open, revealing his bulge, contained behind navy briefs. A quick glance downward revealed what he already knew—that his cock was a respectable length and thickness, clearly outlined by the clinging material.

"Take them off."

Well, he had to change before he left the theater. He pushed the pants down from his hips, pulling them from his muscular legs. Feeling faintly ridiculous, he shed his socks as well. The worn wooden floor abraded the soles of his feet, gritty and warm under his toes.

"Great legs. Do you work out?"

"I run," Billy said shortly, and was silent for a moment as the history behind those two words filled his head. Run, Billy, run...away from the people who aren't like you, who don't understand. Run, fast and far, along the beach, along the road, over muddy trails through golden fall woods. Run with rasping breath, heaving chest, burning thighs, but keep going, until your head clears, and your body is beautiful and weightless and you eat the miles beneath your pounding feet. Now, he ran for the love of it, for the exercise and how it shaped his body, but the first mile of any run was an exorcism of his turbulent years.

"It shows. Oh, does it ever show!"

There was an edge of tension in her voice, a hint of avarice, as if she wanted him. And she did want him, Billy realized. She was there, uncomfortable, hot, probably dirty, just to watch him; a private performance, here in the basement, on the worn boards never trod by any other performer, not in that sense. He swelled, his chest expanding, his back straight, those sturdy runner's legs planted solid, a presence, someone to be looked at.

"Your time for talking is past," he said. "Now you watch me."

He didn't wait for an answer, but turned his back, clenching his asscheeks so they stood out like round rubber melons. Cupping his cock, he pressed it back against his body, feeling the friction. He gyrated a couple of times, then went into a quick fucking rhythm, as if he were pounding a faceless woman, impaling her on his cock, watching it slide back and forth in her wet cunt.

Turning around, he sat down, his legs planted wide. One hand still pressed his cock. Its tip reared above the elastic of his briefs, pressing against his belly. He pulled down the briefs enough that his cock was unencumbered. Freed from the clinging briefs, it jutted out proudly from his groin. Billy ran his fingers lightly up and down its warm surface, tracing the pattern of veins, running his fingertips around the bulbous head.

He cocked an eyebrow in the direction of the curtain. "Like what you see? Is it making your little pussy cream in anticipation? Are your panties bunched and sodden between your thighs?"

There was no answer, but his unseen watcher's concentration was so thick, so palpable that he wondered if she were breathing.

Billy raised his hips enough to pull the briefs down, dragging them along his thighs and kicking them away. They skidded across the floor, coming to rest a few inches in front of the curtain. He settled back down, thighs akimbo, and grasped his cock firmly,

"Go on," he said, in a low voice. "Take them. Sniff them. Find out what I smell like. Imagine what you could be doing if you came out from your hiding place."

He waited, pumping his veined shaft up and down a few times. The heel of his hand pushed back on the downstroke, firmly frotting his clit with the base. He was hot and horny, even if *she* wasn't. He wanted to fuck, to get his rocks off, to

plow into a willing wet pussy, to fuck until he came in a roar of
pleasure.

A shuffling noise behind the curtain alerted him. The curtain
bulged, as if the person behind it were changing position—
maybe to make a grab for his underpants, or maybe to spread
her thighs and dip one, two, even three fingers in between. Billy
saw a small hand, dusky or tanned, he couldn't tell which in the
dim lighting of the room, creep out like a scuttling creature. It
hesitated, felt around until the fingers touched the sweat-sodden
material of his briefs, then there was a quick clutch, a swift with-
drawal with the prize.

Billy waited, idly pumping his cock. He was so aroused he
knew that once he allowed himself, he would blow in a few brief
and glorious moments, but he wanted to savor this fully.

"Bury your nose in them," he instructed. "Smell my sweat,
my arousal, my sex."

A narrow foot encased in a sleek boot the color of burnished
walnut, poked out underneath the curtain. A second followed,
and from the angle, Billy could tell that her thighs were spread
wide, no doubt for easy access to her cunt. The need to have
something of hers was overpowering.

"Throw me your panties," he said. "Now."

A pair of lilac bikini panties scudded across the floor, wadded
into a small ball at his feet. He reached down and spread them
out: nothing exotic, only simple cotton. He inspected the crotch,
where a glistening smear told its own tale. One hand held them
to his nose while the other continued to pump his cock, faster
now, the urgency roiling up in him. She smelled tangy and sharp,
with the slightest hint of soap in there. So she'd washed herself
before hiding here—as if she was expecting someone to bury his
face in her cunt, to run his tongue around her lips, tongue-lash
her clit until she came.

He stilled his movements, and the noise filtering down from upstairs was blessedly quiet, only for a moment, but long enough for him to hear her soft panting and the unmistakable sound of squelching fingers. Billy could picture her: legs outspread; fingers moving fast, slipping and sliding in her copious juices; head thrown back, breasts heaving, thighs as taut and tense as steel wire as she drove herself up, riding on her fingers until her orgasm broke over her.

The visual was enough to loosen his self-control. Groaning, he pumped his cock harder, faster, until his fist was a flying blur. His own climax crashed over him, a juddering series of peaks that left him gasping for breath and acutely aware that he had yelled loudly enough to be heard in the auditorium upstairs. Gently, he pressed down on his cock, seeking the rippling aftershocks.

He dragged in a deep breath to calm himself, letting his body wind down. Sweat sheened his body and his hair clung limply to his head. Naked, he walked over to the curtain and grasped it tightly.

"That was only the appetizer," he said, when he could trust his voice not to shake. "I'm going to count to three and then we'll start on our entree."

Grinning, he heard a frantic shuffle and the expensive leather boots disappeared from underneath the curtain.

"One."

Fast breathing and the sound of rustling cloth.

"Two."

The clatter of a chair hitting the floor.

"Three."

The click of a latch and a door slamming. Running feet.

Shit. He flung back the curtain to see the green metal door of a fire exit. Shit. A dozen chairs and a spilled bottle of disinfectant. The acrid stench overrode the smell of her cunt. Shit. He flung open the door, cautiously aware of his nudity. There was only a dark back alley, quiet and cold, a dingy pile of snow from the last blizzard and a pall of exhaust fumes.

She was gone.

Billy slammed the door and walked back into his dressing room. He looked around for his briefs before he realized his mystery woman must have taken them. Dragging on his 501s, he carefully tucked his cock away. Disappointment coursed through him, a letdown far harder than the milky applause that normally greeted his act. This was a heavy boulder that filled his stomach, expanding into his chest, driving out the warmth of his orgasm.

Billy returned to his mirror and stared at his reflection. His ruddy face stared back at him. Reaching for the whiskey, he chugged a hefty slug from the bottle. As he put it down, his eyes were drawn to a crumpled wad of lilac material off to one side on the floor. Retrieving her panties, he buried his nose in the crotch and inhaled.

There were still three more nights to run in this town.

GLASS

Nobilis Reed

The glass dildo, this time. Yes, definitely the glass. Mira unlocked the bottom drawer and selected the hard transparent shape from the jumble of torpedoes and plastic phalluses and laid it on the desk in front of her.

A gentle curve, a pleasant shade of blue, a few tiny bubbles trapped inside: it could almost pass for a work of art. She smiled at the thought of just leaving it on the shelf alongside the walkie-talkie and the heavy ring of keys. Would anyone say anything? She doubted it.

The couple on her monitor stopped kissing and pulled at each other's clothes. Mira looked up. It wouldn't be long now, but where was that damned lube? Bit by bit, their bodies came into view. They were beautiful, both of them. Every Friday they showed up, performed their *pas de deux*, and left again. She had invented a hundred stories to explain their presence in the depths of the darkened parking garage. Not for the first time, she thanked the nameless engineer who'd invented night-vision video cameras.

She leaned back in her chair, pulled open two buttons of her blouse, and moved one hand into the gap. Fridays always meant watching the couple in the parking lot, so on Fridays Mira always wore the loose bra. Her fingers slipped between the fabric and her skin, crawling toward the sensitive focus. She stroked and squeezed her nipple, watching the couple on her screen.

They were fit and athletic. She could imagine them playing tennis or golf. On Friday, however, they played an entirely different sport, and she was the only spectator.

She hiked up her skirt and slid her panties to the side. Forget the lube. She was dripping. Her fingers danced along the delicate skin, and she drew a sharp breath. Yes, forget the lube. She snatched the dildo from the desk. The cool, hard glass slid effortlessly between her pussy lips. She moaned. Part of her wanted to lean back, close her eyes, and just concentrate on pleasure, but she couldn't stop watching. Mira matched the movements on the screen with her hands, letting their thrusts control her own.

She raised one leg and propped her foot on the desk, causing her sex to open wider. Her other hand shifted from her breast to her clit. Mira rubbed circles, letting the skin of her hood slide over the sensitive nub. Her breathing deepened, quiet moans escaping from her throat with each trembling exhalation. The pale blue dildo disappeared into her cunt again and again, in a gradually increasing tempo.

On the monitor, the lovers tangled themselves in each other's bodies, their hands and mouths roaming. Mira's imagination filled in the details the camera left out: the smell of sweat, the heat radiating from flushed skin, the feel of goose bumps under fingertips.

As her passion reached its peak, Mira shifted the angle of the dildo, using the knob at its tip to bring firm pressure on the sensitive upper wall of her cunt. Her cry of ecstasy reverberated in the tiny office. Her body twitched and spasmed with a powerful orgasm.

As the couple on the screen disengaged, Mira put her clothes back in order. A few antiseptic wipes removed the slippery evidence from the vinyl seat of the chair and disinfected the glass dildo before she locked it in the drawer again. She had to lock everything up for the night, and she wanted to get home on time.

Chris wrapped the overcoat around his body with a smile. It was always this way. It seemed such a cliché to use the stereo-typical pervert's garment, but the fact was that it was the best tool for his purpose. Its bulk and dark color hid him well in the shadows, but being seen walking around in it wouldn't attract attention.

"I'm going out for a walk, honey!"

"Have fun!"

He closed the door behind him and checked his watch. It shouldn't be long, but he didn't need to hurry. His favorite window wasn't far.

A whistle came to his lips as he walked. It wasn't a feigned nonchalance, because at this hour no one else would be out for a stroll in his quiet suburban neighborhood. No, this was a whistle of anticipation, an expression of the brightness of spirit that was rising in his chest. He was the luckiest man on earth, and he just couldn't help letting it out.

After about a block, he came to a small playground. The chains and bars of the equipment were silent, of course, their most recent users in bed hours before. Moonlight threw his shadow across a spring-mounted cartoon worm, then a teeter-totter, then a geodesic dome.

At the far end, Chris turned onto a jogging path that wound

around behind the houses. On either side, rows of bushes and evergreens screened the path from the backyards: the perfect cover.

He knew his spot well, and even though the moonlight threw confusing stripes of light across his path, he found it without any difficulty: a small break in the bushes, a gap caused by stunted growth in one of the hemlocks. Beyond it lay a backyard, adorned with a small decorative pond and a vegetable garden, and beyond that, a wall, and in that wall was the window. The slope up to the path where he stood put him at eye level with it. No drapes adorned it, no blinds protected the privacy of its owners.

He shoved his hands into the pockets of the overcoat. They had, of course, been prepared for just this sort of activity. The left pocket had been cut out, and a slit cut in the liner, leaving his hand free to roam underneath the coat. He slipped his hand under the waistband of his sweats and gave his cock, already hard from anticipation, a preparatory stroke.

His right hand closed around a small pair of binoculars and raised them to his eyes. A twitch of his fingers brought the window into focus. The bed was situated directly across the room from the window, the perfect stage for the performance that was about to unfold.

A blonde woman came into view, dressed in a blue silk bathrobe. The thin material caressed her body, revealing subtle, delicate curves. She had the body of a dancer, taut smooth muscles stretched over long bones.

A car turned the corner up the street, illuminating the gaps between the houses. The beams flashed and then died as the car pulled up into the driveway. Chris checked his watch: showtime.

The sound of a car door opening, then closing, and more

faintly, the door to the house doing the same reached his ears. Moments later, the bedroom door opened, revealing the other actress in the evening's entertainment. She was shorter than the first, with a long, dark braid.

The blonde embraced the woman and quickly stripped off her mannish blue shirt and sports bra, revealing a large, luscious pair of breasts. The bathrobe likewise came off, exposing all of the blonde's creamy skin. They kissed hungrily, their embrace a tango of squeezes and caresses.

Chris wanted to let the rhythm of the strokes on his cock match the frenetic pace of the lovemaking he was watching, but he refrained, limiting himself to long, slow squeezes. He knew the habits of these women, and their appetites would not be sated quickly. He savored every moment.

The last of the dark woman's clothes fell away, and they climbed onto the bed. For a while, the blonde rubbed the dark woman's body, and ran her fingers through the curly thatch of hair at her crotch. Before a minute had passed, however, the dark woman took her partner's face in her hands, kissed her passionately on the lips, and then pushed her down toward her spreading legs.

Chris could not see what the blonde was doing, but he could imagine it. His mind filled in every detail: the musky scent of woman, the moans and cries of ecstasy, even the tiny sounds of tongue on pussy.

Then something brushed past his leg. His heart leapt into his throat and he looked down to catch a glimpse of a furry white tail. A dog. He blew out a relieved breath.

Then, faintly, from down the path, came a voice. "Frosty! Frosty!" The voice became louder, clearer. Someone was coming, someone looking for the dog. Chris slid down, pushed into the bushes, down into the deepest shadows.

"Frosty! Fr—oh, my god…"

The owner of the voice was a man, a bit younger than Chris from the sound, but definitely not a boy. He stopped right where Chris had been standing, his slippered feet only inches from where Chris was hiding. He knew he risked discovery by doing so, but he had to look up.

The man was dressed in boxers and a T-shirt, bright white in the moonlight. He whistled in appreciation at what he was seeing. The shadows did not reveal much to Chris, but he could tell this fledgling voyeur was enjoying the show, too. He stood in mesmerized silence.

Chris cursed his bad luck, but found himself unable to take his eyes away from the younger man's gradually protruding shorts. It was hard to judge scale from the strange angle and the poor lighting, but even so, the man had to be spectacularly endowed.

Clearly thinking himself alone, the interloper slid his hand up and down over the front of his boxers, then under the waistband to jack himself in earnest. He didn't stop to savor the experience, but rather powered into it, entranced by the vision before him.

Jealousy warred with arousal in Chris's mind. The intruder was watching a sight that he felt should be his alone to enjoy, yet there was a certain vicarious thrill to seeing the other man becoming more and more aroused. What else was there to do? He simply stayed where he was, letting the negative emotions drain out of him. After all, there would be a next time.

He knew, more or less, what the man would be seeing. Chris could see it in his mind's eye, from many long observations. After the massage, the blonde would spend long minutes eating the brunette's pussy, driving her to an ecstatic, thrashing orgasm.

After that, a toy would come out. It might be a strap-on, or a double dildo, or a Swedish vibrator, or silken red ropes. There might or might not be a blindfold involved, but no matter what happened, the blonde was going to get fucked.

With a quiet groan, the man came, and Chris could hear the soft rustle as the spurts of come disturbed the branches above him. Then, suddenly, he was gone, running back down the path the way he had come. Something had spooked him. Whether it was the notice of the women inside the house, or even the dog, Chris could not say.

He rolled over onto his back and brought his binoculars back up to his eyes. The women were cuddling now, clearly finished with whatever round of amorous play they had been involved in. The light inside the bedroom snapped off.

He sighed and put the binoculars back in his pocket. There would be next week.

Lucy climbed out of bed and plodded into the bathroom. She didn't need to clean up, not really, but a warm shower always relaxed her when sleep wouldn't come on its own. No soap, no shampoo, she just adjusted the water to almost all the way hot and let it flow.

Only it didn't work. Instead of relaxing her, it just made things worse. Her hands slid over her slick skin as she imagined her lover's hands making the same motions—such talented hands, knowledgeable hands, familiar with every curve, every secret place of pleasure.

Nothing else to do, she thought to herself, as she turned off the water. A soft sound came through the door, a quiet moan of satisfaction. Lucy ran her hand over the glass shower enclosure, clearing the fog away so she could see through the open door into the bedroom.

The moonlight streaming through her window threw dramatic shadows across the two shapes lying on her bed. The man was curled up with the woman, spoon fashion, with one hand holding their bodies together as he thrust gently from behind. The woman clutched the sheets and arched her back, her body twitching with the aftershock of a powerful but quiet orgasm.

When she had stilled, he took one slim feminine ankle and raised it up and around his body as he rose. With her flexible body, she did not complain. With her now on her back, he could move more powerfully, eliciting a new set of sounds, this time from his own throat.

Lucy found her own breathing rising in sync with his grunts of effort, feeling each powerful thrust almost as if it were her body he was fucking. She wasn't supposed to be watching them, it wasn't time, it hadn't been planned, but she was transfixed, unable to move forward to join them, unable to pull back and give them some privacy. She wiped at the glass again.

Her hand found her breast. She squeezed, imagining that cock pounding between her own legs, those hands on her own body, losing herself in the border between fantasy and reality. When he growled, then shouted, as his climax wracked his body, she found her own body responding as well.

The orgasm released her from her reverie, and she stumbled out of the shower and into the bedroom. There was no chance to hide what she had been doing, but the two lovers on her bed didn't care. They greeted her with friendly, inviting smiles of satisfaction.

"Hey, Lucy!" said Mira. "You won't believe what happened to Chris while he was out watching!"

SLEEPING BEAUTY

Malcolm Ross

Some people might think that the only ones with sexual secrets are those having affairs, or single folks with wild lives that involve a different bed partner (or two) every night. But me? I'm a happily married man (eleven years, thank you very much), but I have a dirty little secret: I like to watch my wife, Inez, sleep. Well, "like" is a bit of an understatement. Watching her at rest turns me on, makes my dick come alive.

First off, let me tell you that Inez is gorgeous; she has a model-beautiful face, with her pitch black, shiny, silky hair that spills halfway down her back, full lips, big breasts and an ass that curves so perfectly I could cry. She has blazing green eyes that I love looking into, but love even more when I can't see them but just know they're there, waiting until they can spark once again. She works in HR for a major gym, and considers staying in shape, keeping her long hair lush and her appearance at its best part of her job requirements, though she's the kind of woman who loves to pamper herself. My point is, she's always stunning, even when she's just standing around in sweats (for her, that usually means going topless with a cozy pair of black sweatpants that end at her muscular calves). She's got a closet full of clothes that cling perfectly to her body, by designers whose names mean nothing to me. But to me, she's at her most beautiful when she's asleep, hair spilling around her, her small body rising and falling, curled in such a way that her ass looks even rounder, utterly caught off guard.

It's not that I don't love her when she's awake, especially during sex, with her writhing on top of me, her breasts bouncing in my face—when her nipples aren't shoved in my mouth for me to suckle. It's not an either/or situation. But when she's in repose, I just can't help wanting to take her, to rub my cock all over her, to bring her to life just like the mythical Sleeping Beauty. Instead of my lips, I'd use my cock to fuck her awake, but slowly, giving me enough time to savor her sleeping form.

I discovered my fetish—if that's what you want to call it— when I was pulling an all-nighter for an article I'd been procrastinating on writing. I kept staring at my screen, frantically checking the word count, then getting up and staring out at the moon. Knowing that Inez was tucked away under our sumptuous comforter, the one she'd had to convince me was worth three hundred dollars, her naked body lost in dreams, made me jealous that she never had to take her job home with her, while I often wound up staying up until the wee hours to complete a last-minute assignment.

I used to work as an editor at a magazine, so the rhythm of my work weeks was pretty steady; I had some long nights, but usually only three or four, all clustered together. Being freelance meant being permanently on call, like a doctor, and while I could technically decline assignments, I couldn't really afford to, and I prided myself on being able to meet any deadline. I'd gotten pretty used to using a combination of coffee, cigarettes, Twizzlers, and infomercials to get me through the rough patches where the words seemed to die on my fingertips, but that night none of my usual vices was working. And then I discovered Inez, asleep.

I still had at least an hour of work left. I was pacing the house, and for some reason, decided to look in on her. I paused and truly looked at my wife, at her freshly painted nails, their bright coral glowing against the white sheet, her long lashes, her lips devoid of lipstick or gloss but still so lush and tender. I peeled the sheet down enough to ogle the firm lines of her back, the curve of her ass, the one I so often held in my hands as she rode me, or spanked when she wanted me to pretend she'd been naughty. Before that night, I'd always just crawled right into bed alongside her, so eager to join my body to hers, to feel her body heat against me, to maybe invade her dreams, to speed ahead to the part where I woke up next to her.

I wondered if, during those moments she got crazy and told me she was too "fat," I could explain to her how perfect she was, completely bare, without even trying. My two long-term exes had insisted on sleeping in my oversized T-shirts and their panties, even after sex; only on rare occasions would they strip down to their birthday suits. Inez, on the other hand, only wore anything to bed when we had company or were visiting someone, and even then, it was always just a silky wisp of a thing. Her penchant for nighttime nudity was another reason I loved her, and seeing her so exposed unleashed a rabid kind of lust in me.

I knelt down, my dick rising in my boxers as I peered at the crack of her ass. I'd been inside her there a few times over the years—neither of us was all that into anal sex—but had never really gotten up close and personal. I had to take my cock out of my shorts then because it was getting painful to wait. She'd never know the difference, right? Oh, I should add that Inez is a very heavy sleeper. She's slept through arguments, sirens, meals, even an earthquake once. Like everything else in her life, when she throws herself into something, she throws herself 100 percent. My ex before her, Tracy, she of the T-shirt as sleepwear, had been such a light sleeper that every little noise woke her, and consequently, me as well. But my Inez had to be shaken awake or blasted into the day by her blaring alarm, which she'd set to sound like a barking dog, a noise I'd never fully gotten used to.

So I knew she wouldn't wake up suddenly and find me beating off. And if she did, what harm was there in what I was doing? She was my wife, not some stranger, and I knew she masturbated in the shower, while she knew I usually got myself off at night if we didn't wind up fooling around. It was never an issue for us, so I only had the mildest pang of guilt as I pumped my cock while letting my eyes dance over her sleeping form. Her body rose high and fell, and twice she let a few mumbled words of Spanish slip out. Her parents are Chilean immigrants; she grew up speaking both Spanish and English. Though she considers English her first language, after a few drinks or when she's very tired, she sometimes reverts to Spanish; she apparently did the same when she was asleep.

I didn't understand the language, but could recognize its mellifluous beauty. I was grateful because I didn't want to know her secrets, not all of them; it was bad enough that I was ogling her like this, yet the very slight tinge of guilt I felt turned me on as much as it chastened me. I inched closer, as close as I could get without actually touching her. She sighed, mumbled something in neither English nor Spanish, but simply the language of the sleeping, then turned over so she was facing me. If she opened her eyes even a little, she'd see my naked cock, hard and aimed right at her. I envisioned myself coming all over her pretty face, something I'd never done but had certainly contemplated in fantasy. Once, I'd even whispered the suggestion to her while in the middle of doing it doggy-style. She'd whimpered, turned on by the idea of it, but we'd both gotten carried away and come soon thereafter.

This was kind of like that, and I wondered what she was dreaming about, because her tongue reached out to lick her lips. I recognized "Si," as she twisted around in what seemed to be a sex dream. Was I the star? I forced my hand to still as I walked to the foot of the bed and flung the covers all the way off of her. I stared at the bright, sparkly hot-pink polish on her toes, her tanned legs, roasted to the most gorgeous chestnut by the sun, legs I knew were silky smooth. I couldn't see her entire pussy, but recognized those sweet lips peeking out from between her legs, and the edging of fuzz starting to grow there.

Knowing I couldn't touch her wasn't a hardship, even though, had she woken, I'd gladly have joined her in bed, work be damned. I welcomed the opportunity to watch her, to look my fill, to notice nuances of her skin I'd never seen before, to observe the way she breathed, to remind myself of her beauty. When I did finally come, out of some odd form of respect, I went in the bathroom to do it.

But that night started a pattern, albeit an irregular one. It's not like I spy on my sleeping wife every night. Most nights I join her in slumber, both of us nodding off, our bodies tangled in some complicated manner involving feet and hands and necks and hips. Feeling her soft breaths beat against me is something I treasure. Yet I've come to look forward to the nights she has to crash early, or I'm called upon to perform another all-nighter. "I'm heading up," she told me the other night as we sat curled on the couch watching the news. I pulled her close for a kiss but didn't join her, though I wasn't really watching anymore. I was anticipating what would happen after she got under the covers.

"Don't stay up too late," Inez said with a smile as she sashayed up the stairs.

I waited, even dozed off for a few minutes before I climbed up to our room. I heard her tidy snores before I got there. What I found made my heart beat faster; her hand was tucked between her legs, as if she'd fallen asleep after making herself come. You think you know someone as well as they know themselves after so many years, but maybe I'd misread her words; maybe "Don't stay up too late" had meant, "Hurry upstairs so you can fuck me before I crash." I wondered if it had, if she'd thought of me while jerking off, or some man she'd seen that day at work, or a celebrity. I wondered if she'd given herself the kind of orgasm that makes the world stop, makes life seem so complete you wonder why you don't do it every minute of every day, or if it had been the kind of climax that's incomplete in some way, pleasant enough, but missing something...like my dick.

I wanted to slide my hand alongside hers, to touch her, but instead I just watched, waiting for her to move, to give me a glimpse between her legs. She only does that when I really beg, not so much self-conscious as impatient when I take too long to savor her beauty. "Give me your tongue already, baby," she'll beg in a way I can't resist. So now I watched and waited, not rushing to reach for my cock but letting my gaze do the dirty work.

I was implanting the memory of her like this on my brain, her so utterly different from her usual feral wildness. I'd already racked up plenty of nights standing before her, minutes stolen from the night so I could see her. There was still a hint of her moxie; even at rest her eyeballs roamed behind her closed lids. There's a hunger to her that doesn't stop just because she's in her own dreamworld. I had a hunger, too, one I was tormenting myself by not slaking. There have been times I've woken her in the middle of the night, silently asking her with my hard cock for a quick fuck in the dark. I could have done so, and she'd probably have gotten wet for me; it doesn't take much with her.

Instead I drew out the beautiful, blessed agony; the frustration of wanting her, seeing her so near, yet so far from my touch. I stood as close as I could to her and slowly worked my cock in my hand, watching it practically bursting from its skin. It was sex in slo-mo—solo sex, but yet it somehow made me feel intimately connected with her. Maybe she was dreaming of my dick, maybe she subconsciously knew what was going on.

When I knew my orgasm was imminent, I walked away. What Inez didn't know wouldn't hurt her, and I wanted to savor my own private pervy fairy tale, of a true sleeping beauty who would wake up in mere hours. I jerked off in the shower, watching the results of my viewing splatter the tiles.

I took a hot shower, letting the practically scalding water seep into my skin, but it didn't wash away the image in my mind of my wife in repose. I went back to work, my fingers suddenly flying over the keys, the words racing to get out. Not only was Inez a source of arousal for me, she was also my muse. I smoked a very satisfying cigarette when I was done, then gingerly got into bed next to her, shutting my own eyes, inhaling the strawberry scent of her perfume, the unique aroma of her body, as I let one sense overtake another.

I haven't told her yet, but I plan to someday. Will it affect her sleep? Will she be turned on by my secret nighttime viewing, or will she suddenly think I'm not to be trusted? Will her knowing make me want to watch her less, or more? When I decide to truly awaken my beauty, I'll find out.

THE THEORY OF ORCHIDS

L. A. Mistral

I t all seemed to happen by accident. It wasn't as if Gina started out this way. It almost took her by surprise. The first time she didn't even know she was doing it. She remembered she was on the Metro in D.C., on her way to the Smithsonian, to the Sackler Gallery, in fact, for an exhibit of Sasanian gold. She was leafing through the catalog of gold necklaces with Dionysus and large, silver serving platters depicting the full-hipped Aphrodite at play in banquets and the hearts of lovers, and preoccupied with the petal-nippled river-nymphs on silver drinking horns. She didn't even notice them looking at first. But they were looking at her. Actually, they were looking at her lap.

Gina looked around. Were they looking at someone else? Why her? Did she have a tear in her dress? Gina had worn a smart-looking, navy blue skirt with the hem coming to midthigh and a white blouse and coordinated waistcoat to complete her ensemble. Gina had always caught attention, although she never admitted it to herself. Her hair was the color of an Umbrian merlot and when the sun caught it just right, shimmered with flecks of gold filigree. Gina's eyes were as big as an amaryllis in full bloom. But it was the deep-blue color that held the gaze of others, that and how the dramatic slope of her eyebrows intensified the glance of her eyes. But she was so shy that she never admitted to herself how much she aroused others.

It was time to break out a little. She wanted to take it slow, going to public places in short, measured intervals, looking a few people in the eye at first and saying "Hello" to a passerby.

Now, on the Metro, she glanced up for a moment. Two or three people, two men and one woman, she recalled, were still staring at her. Polite, to be sure, they glanced down when their eyes met. The strange thing was that the more they stared the more excited she became. Her heart quickened its pace and her breath seemed to bang out of her breast. Then Gina looked down at her skirt. The hem had caught on a rivet in the seat and raised way up her thighs. Her skirt had risen so high that the crotch of her evening blue panties was clearly visible, bulging with the high mound of her hyacinth pussy. She blushed immediately.

Then she did something totally out of character. She slumped down in her seat and spread her legs even farther apart. Her panties were so wet, they were translucent, and her pussy blossomed like an orchid big as the moon between her legs. She felt shamed all right, but that wasn't all she felt. She was so aroused, her whole body hummed. She also felt strangely strong, vibrant. She unfastened the skirt in a leisurely way and smoothed it down. She almost felt let down, disappointed, except that she liked it way too much. Except that her panties were soaking wet.

It wasn't even as if they were leering. Their gazes seemed more appreciative than exploitive. They didn't want to control her. They just wanted to cherish her.

It was the looking that aroused her. She couldn't deny the

shame she felt at exposing herself, but she wouldn't deny the euphoria either. *Maybe we shy girls are simmering inside,* she thought. She felt like she had accidentally lost her virginity. She was stepping into a new country.

Now, she was no novice. She couldn't pretend. She'd done her share of practice runs. She'd hiked her skirt on buses and the short train rides she'd taken. She'd always gotten the response she'd hoped for. But that only whet her appetite. Now she was ready for something more.

A vacation in a warm climate was the perfect answer. She decided on a resort in the north coast of Florida, just big enough to offer an introduction to sailing and small enough to provide a feeling of intimacy. She wasn't looking for crowds. She was looking for intimacy. That's what the brochure said and that's what she wanted.

When she arrived at St. Marys, Florida, she knew she'd chosen well. Only six or seven small, whitewashed bungalows meandered on the shoreline and there was a pier with one forty-five-foot sailboat bobbing on the surface of the green-gilded water. It was dusk when she arrived and the sun slanted across the palm trees behind her, making streaks of gold and crimson in the water.

Her hosts, Gail and Dan, welcomed her. They were an older couple, friendly but professional in their introductions. "It's a beautiful setting. Quiet and very private. We let our guests do as they please here. We will go sailing tomorrow at nine."

"Oh, yes, one more thing," Gail said, reaching out for Gina's hand. "It's a custom in the islands," she said, placing a flower in Gina's hair. "In the Antilles, a welcome gift is palm oil and an orchid. The adults-only cruise ships that pass by here drop some off for us." Gail then brushed a scented oil across Gina's chin and her cheek and brushed some in her hair. "It's a blessing, really," Gail said.

Gina was touched by the gift and lifted the flower from her hair to smell it. It had the earthy, musky smell of the mangrove forest as well as the sweetness of cinnamon and vanilla.

She placed the orchid in water while she unpacked, and then, when she'd changed from jeans into a light, short dress, someone knocked at her door. When she opened it, she was surprised to find a young man standing there, bag in hand, looking confused.

"I'm so sorry," he said, "I must have the wrong cabin. I'm supposed to be in bungalow six."

"This is number five, I think," she said, suddenly uncertain. She started to doubt herself. "Come inside while I check," she said, forcing herself to look at him straight in the eyes. He smiled right at her.

He was younger than she, maybe twenty-two or twenty-three by the look of his careless hair and sparse beard. Gina wondered what his face might feel like next to hers. *Would it scratch or tickle?* she wondered. She looked at her keys. "Yes, this is cabin five. Yours must be over there," she said, pointing.

"So sorry," he said, frowning. "I didn't mean to bother you."

His smile and shy manner disarmed her. She decided to take a chance. "On vacation?" she asked, looking into his rich, chocolate eyes.

Appreciating the conversation after a long flight, he answered, "Running away, really," the corners of his mouth turning up in a tiny smile.

Gina was feeling a bit playful. "You mean AWOL from the Army? Or maybe a fugitive from prison?"

"Sort of," he said with a straight face. "But not as exciting. I'm running away from my lab at the university. I'm a horticulturist." He held out his hand.

"Hard work?" Gina asked, their hands lingering over each

other just a little too long.

"I'm studying the power of seeing on orchids."

"How so?" she said, now curious. His smooth mouth seemed friendly and she imagined how it would feel if he pulled on her nipples with his teeth.

"Flowers respond to looks of love," he said. "It's an extension of Heisenberg's Uncertainty Theory."

"Now you've done it," she said, teasing him, his dark eyes, smooth skin and easy manner intriguing her. "You have to explain that!" She also wondered what it would be like to tease his nipples with her own teeth.

He was embarrassed to be lecturing, but since she'd asked, he said, "That just means that we change whatever we look at." Gina was really hooked now, remembering how she liked to be watched. She had to know more about this guy. Much more.

Gina introduced herself and took his hand. "Nick, and pleased to meet you," he said, his hand warm. They held on just long enough to become embarrassed. His touch warmed her whole body. She was glad now for the warm breeze that flapped beneath her short skirt, tickling her pantyless pussy.

"And cabin five must be to the right," she added, just to get the detail out of the way. She leaned against the doorway and invited his eyes to play with the hem of her skirt. She shifted her legs to accommodate his gaze and his eyes flipped her hem above her waist and explored the twists of her pussy hairs, petting them until they purred.

He became embarrassed. "And now I'll leave before I bore you to death," he said. Nick moved to the door to leave and Gina followed him.

It was early evening now and the moon had risen. Its light was as pale as Gina's skin and filtered through the dark forest by the nearby water flooding them with currents and streams of silver and opal. The dull throb of the sailboat's lifting and dipping gave an eerie, strangely sensual rhythm to the atmosphere. Just then, a slight movement caught their eyes: two lovers were silhouetted on the sailboat. "It must be Gail and Dan," Gina told Nick. Nick put his finger up to his full, friendly lips and squinted into the silhouettes. Neither he nor Gina said a word. They were mesmerized, enraptured by the movements of the figures and how they were shown against the backdrop of moonlight and the mangrove trees.

Standing on the deck, Gail and Dan were both clearly naked and clearly excited. Dan's cock was fully erect and Gail was kneeling in front of him stroking it. Gail's breasts were not large, but her nipples were so erect and long that they stuck out like crescent moons. Dan leaned into her as his cock slid deeper and deeper inside her mouth. Nick and Gina could see the whole length of his cock as it came out again. Dan's long cock slid in and out of Gail's mouth faster and faster. They were so close, Nick and Gina could hear Gail's deep-hearted moans and Dan's cries of ecstasy. As Dan neared orgasm, Gail lifted his stiff cock into the air and pumped it hard with her hand. Against the moonlight, Nick and Gina saw his cock spurt into the air and Gail lick the full length of him. After a moment, Gail leaned back and when she raised her cunt into the air, Dan pushed into her and they embraced for one long moment.

Gina was breathing hard by now and leaned against Nick. She felt his cock even through his jeans and her short dress. Without really knowing it, they were pressing into each other and Gina closed her eyes and felt warmed and comforted by Nick's willing cock rubbing against the crack of her ass. When she opened her eyes again, Dan and Gail had turned their heads toward Nick and Gina. Neither Gina nor Nick knew whether Dan and Gail saw them; but as Gail and Dan left the boat and passed within a few yards of them, Gail seemed to wink at Gina with her right eye. Gina could have sworn that the other woman's ass winked at her too.

"I hope to see you tomorrow, for boating," Nick told Gina, suddenly aware of their quick but intense intimacy. "Me, too," she said.

Gina wasn't disappointed the next day when Nick arrived to get his sailing lesson. No one mentioned the events of the previous evening. Gina was prepared for sailing and so was Gail. Gail's bra and Brazilian-cut briefs were barely a breath against her skin, and equally transparent. Her small nipples brightened in the fresh air as they left the dock. Dan's strong thighs and hefty biceps were well used in controlling the sails and rigging. Nick was built more like a swimmer than a scientist. His broad shoulders accented his slender waist. His grace trumped his muscles. Gina couldn't help but imagine him without his swim trunks.

Gina was equally prepared with a white suit that barely stretched over her breasts and just covered her hibiscus flower of pussy hair. Her suit only accented her full hips and breasts. Her pinot noir nipples showed through the suit dark and large as begonias. Everyone on board was wondering what it would feel like to sip them.

A cruise liner approached them while Nick explained his research to Gail. "The more we admire orchids, the more intense their color," he told her. "The more we cherish something with our eyes, the more it flourishes."

"Just by our looking at it?" Gail asked, taken aback.

"Exactly," Nick said. "Our attention has a force all its own. It changes both who we are and what we look at. Our watching changes everything."

"Like you both changed us last night?" Gail asked, still smiling.

"You saw us?" they said, not so much alarmed as excited.

Gail replied with a sly smile, "Of course, that was half the fun!"

Just then, the cruise liner edged away from them. To keep alongside, Dan had to change his direction. "They might think we're pirates..." he said, half-joking, "...given the recent news reports."

He began to strip off his shorts. Gail reached back and unhooked the thin line of her bikini top and handed it to him. Her taut-nippled breasts burst out like a sunrise. "I guess we'd better show off our friendly intentions," Dan explained.

Meanwhile, Gina and Nick were getting friendly them-selves. Gina stood by the mast, holding on to it more as an invitation than for balance. Nick walked behind her, nestled his chin inside her neck, and whispered a hot greeting heavily into her ear. Reaching back, Gina hugged Nick closer and pressed back up against him with the length of her body. Gina sighed a loud, long, low moan. She bent forward and stripped down her slender briefs all the way to the deck and then kicked them off. Nick slipped the edge of one hand inside her cunt and cupped another hand around her breast.

Gina's pussy felt as plush as a cashmere sweater. Her nipples caught both the breeze and the gaze of her admirers on board the cruise liner. The passengers waved and her nipples waved back. She pressed back into Nick and felt his swollen cock urging itself into her crack. The head of his cock surged between her legs like a warm, wet tide and pressed against her again and again. Unable to resist her begonia-sized nipples, he sucked one and then the other between his lips and then his teeth. The pain was sharp and exquisite and Gina leaned her head back against his cheek. Nick looked at her half-closed eyes and straight into her heart.

Above them, the cruise ship went quiet. There were no whistles, no rude jokes, no cameras. The passengers watched and
the more they watched, the more they were touched. Their eyes
went wide as orchids. There was only silence—silence and the
gracious gravity of eyes astonished and stroking.

Gina felt the charm of their stares, and the weight of their
wonder pressed her over. When she bent over, Gina's pussy
opened like a summer orchard. As he gripped her by the twin
petals of her bottom, he felt a sprinkle on his body. At first he
thought it was a shower, but he smelled the scent of perfume and
palm oil. The passengers aboard the cruise liner were blessing
them with flowers and palm oil. Gina and Nick looked up at
each other, then at the passengers. All they saw was love.

Dan and Gail were doing their share of performing, too. Dan
rubbed his stiff cock between Gail's breasts while she licked
the head of his cock every time he pushed up into her. Nick
and Gina could see his precome shining in the sun. Gina turned
around to see Nick take some of the palm oil that had pooled on
her back and wipe it all over his cock. Then he dipped his cockhead into the mouth of Gina's pussy and slipped it inside and
out. He could see it stretch her pussy lips out and pull them shut
when he withdrew. Her cunt lips licked his cock clean each time.
Everyone else saw the same thing. All of the people watching
held their breath.

Gina banged her hips back and forth against Nick as he
pressed into her more and more quickly. The scent of coconut
oil leaked out of Gina's pussy and filled the air. First Gina came
and then Nick followed with long moans and quick spurts. He
pulled his cock out, and tapping it onto her skin, wrote blank
verse with his come on the small of Gina's back.

Something like a wing drifted down across Gina's back
and she rolled over, facing the passengers. She took the orchid

someone had thrown to her and pushed it inside her swollen pussy. She saw some of the passengers wave. Gina spread her legs farther apart and the brilliant petals of the orchid waved back.

MISSING MICHAEL

M. March

Leo

Michael's standing in front of me and I'm not at all surprised to see him—even though he's been dead seven months now. In fact, I've been seeing a lot of him lately—on crowded city streets, in peaceful little parks, by noisy, nasty nightclubs. I'm thrilled when he shows up in my sex dreams and horrified when he stars in my nightmares.

This time he's in a Chelsea gym, trying to lift a barbell. His brown eyes are practically pinning me to the wall as his massive biceps push upward. He's swimming in sweat, consumed by determination, on fire with a purpose. His dark curly hair is flopping over his headband and his too-big pants are falling slightly below his hips.

I close my eyes and imagine my tongue thrust inside of him, making his asshole silky slick. I want to throw him down on the ground and ride his face from one breathtaking orgasm to the next.

He lets out a loud groan and I wonder for a moment if I've made him come using just my mind, but he hasn't had an orgasm. He's only lifted the barbell.

After a few seconds, he sets the weight down and walks to my right, forever shattering the illusion: from this angle, he doesn't look like Michael at all. His eyes are too close and his chin is too long.

Damn it.

Michael

You know, I hate to see Leo so depressed, but damn if he doesn't look adorable. The first time I saw him pout, all I could think about was how fantastic that pucker would feel wrapped around my dick. And was I right! The first time he went down on me, it was like my cock was sliding between two tiny, fat pillows.

I love his hair too, so thick and soft and shiny. I can see he's gotten a little grayer now and I know that bothers him, but I just think it makes him look more sophisticated.

And his body's still beautiful, though I know he works hard on it, practically living at the gym to keep up that defined chest and that tight little behind that used to fit my dick like it was molded to it.

But lest you think me too shallow, you should know I miss the hugs the most—those big, warm embraces that made me feel more loved than words ever could.

Jeez, I'm sorry to start crying here, but Christ, it's hard, getting to see him only from afar. Still I think I've finally accepted I'm not coming back to Earth. I wish Leo would accept it as well. He needs to move on. He needs to find someone to make him happy again.

Leo

I've just gotten a monster erection.

It happened when Gym Boy took off his shirt. I got this terrible craving to pinch his hard, red nipples and then my dick got huge, swollen beyond belief. I was scared someone would notice it, so I went into the bathroom to take care of myself.

And now as I touch my cock, I can't help but see Gym Boy in swimming trunks. He is kissing me and sticking a finger up my ass and covering my prick with his mouth and I am getting so hard and I am screaming and stroking myself so fast I may have a heart attack. A part of me hopes I will. I need to see Michael again.

Oh god, this feels so good. No, not just good; I am mad with pleasure. I feel like strutting around the gym—no, all of New York—with my giant cock out for every man to see and suck.

I spy a hole in the wall and think it's the perfect size, and before I realize how ridiculous it is, I'm putting my dick in there, and thrusting my hips, and smacking my bare ass. I am not thinking about moving out of our house. I am not worrying about how to turn down that great guy my sister wants me to date; I am not wondering how I will manage to visit my husband's grave without having yet another nervous breakdown.

All I am doing is thinking of Gym Boy.

And then it's over.

And then all I can think about is how Michael is not here to hold me.

I pull up my pants and walk to the mirror. Though I feel less stressed, I certainly don't look it. There are dark circles under my eyes and I can't remember the last time I had a full night's sleep. My cheeks are sunken in because I haven't eaten a decent meal in what feels like forever and my eyes are still puffy from that stupid crying jag I had last night. I was set off by some old movie with George Clooney; I don't even remember the title. Michael loved George and I used to tell Michael he could have sex with him a) if George Clooney ever turned out to be gay and b) if George Clooney ever noticed Michael's existence. Michael said I could have a celebrity lover too, but I never wanted anyone but him.

I clean up and go back outside.

Michael

Boy, my baby's really something, isn't he? Did you see how hard he pounded that wall? Did you see how his sweet little ass turned bright red while he was smacking himself? Did you get a load of how his body shook right before he came and how the cum just shot out of him? I love the way he grunts when he thrusts, the way he loses control completely. If I had been there I would have taken him from behind while he was fucking that wall; I would have licked the back of his neck while he was screaming; I would have whispered sweet encouragement as the fireworks exploded inside his brain; I would have wiped that sweat off his forehead and fucked him for as long as I could, until my thighs were aching, until I was out of breath, until I was fucking spent from the effort of it all.

Oh my Leo, my poor, sweet, Leo—so horny you've taken to masturbating in public restrooms.

I think we need to get you a man.

Leo

Gym Boy is on a treadmill, glistening like the fine jewel he is. His odor is a dizzying combo of musk and sweat and I want to drown in his armpits. I want him to open my ass so wide that it actually hurts. I want him to take away the pain I'm feeling by distracting me with another pain, a safer pain, a pain that has an end to it, rather than this forever gloom. I want Gym Boy's dick to accomplish what all those antidepressants can't.

But no, I think, I could never be with another man. I'm a terrible person for even having these thoughts.

Anyway, why would he want a guy like me, an old, emotional mess? I come with so much baggage it could fill a dozen suitcases.

I look at Gym Boy again and am surprised to see he's smiling at me.

Brian

Hot damn, did I pick the right gym! Just look at that cute guy over there, with those light green eyes and that sexy Roman nose. I mean, okay, he is probably fifty or whatever, but that doesn't bother me; I've always had a thing for older men. God, I love the way he peeks at me and then looks away really quick, like he's doing something naughty and doesn't want to be caught. But I'll catch him. I'll catch him and I'll tie him to my bed and I'll fuck him all night. I'll eat his ass like it's a seven-course meal and suck his nipples like they're a cold milkshake. I'll push his knees up to his ears and shove his cock down my throat.

And then I'll hold him in my arms as we watch the sun come up together.

Leo

Gym Boy is doing sit-ups. I want to hold on to his ankles, see all that determination up close, be a part of his glory.

I close my eyes.

I am putting oil on him and he is moaning, shaking with desire. I tease his asshole with greased-up fingers, tracing the outline slowly. He wants nothing more than for me to stuff all my greasy digits up his ass, but I will not. I will make him suffer, the same way he is making me suffer right now. He holds me tight. He is covering me with his body.

I am letting Michael go.

When I open my eyes, Gym Boy's gone.

I head to the locker room, ready to call it a day.

Brian
He's in front of me. This is my last chance.

"Hey there, I'm Brian."

Leo
He's talking to me. All right. Just stay cool now. This doesn't have to get sexual.

And while I'm saying those words to myself, I accidentally stumble into his arms.

"Oh my god! I'm sorry."

"Don't be," he replies right before he kisses me.

No, don't do this, I want to scream. *Please, just go and find someone who isn't so damaged. You're so beautiful; you could have anybody.*

But I touch his cheeks and I run my fingers through his hair. I know I shouldn't be doing this, so then why does it feel so right?

The past year flashes before my eyes. I see Michael getting thinner, paler, and sicker. I remember how I told him I had this dream once that he was still here twenty years from now. At first, he lets me have this fantasy, but after I mention it for the tenth time he begs, "Please let me go, Leo."

Months after he's died, I'm looking through old scrapbooks and listening to old love songs. I am sorting through mail he will never receive. Friends want to see me, but I have refused them. Michael's parents want to have me over for dinner, but I can't even think about that. I've become a recluse. I'm safe here, in this house that we shared, with the memories that belong to just the two of us. As long as I stay here, I'll always have Michael. But if I go out, if I have fun, I'll be abandoning him and maybe then he'll start abandoning me—stop haunting me. If I go out, I am telling Michael that my life goes on without him, and I don't believe that for a second.

"What are you thinking?" Brian asks, holding his dick in his hands.

I am thinking that he is beautiful but that I can't—

"I promise I won't force you to do anything you're not comfortable with."

If he only knew how much I was comfortable with, how kinky Michael and I used to get, how pain was our language of love. "No, it's not that. It's that—"

It's that the only man I've ever loved is gone and I don't know how to move on.

And that's when it happens: I become a selfish monster.

I cheat on my boyfriend.

Before I grab Brian's dick, I wonder: How does he like it? How long until I learn his natural rhythm? How long until I make him come so fast his head spins?

How long until he leaves me?

How long until I leave him?

Is it worth it to love somebody, when you know it will only end in loss and one of you will be left standing alone?

Brian is on all fours now, waiting for me to enter him. At first, I am scared to even move, but then, slowly, I push my hips against him. And then I move faster, filling more of his ass up with my cock. It is familiar and it is not. It is good and it is terrible. I feel guilty, but also relieved. I close my eyes and yell out, "Oh, Mommy."

Just like I did with Michael.

And Brian cracks up, just like Michael used to. I want to laugh with him, because it is funny, but I can't seem to so much as crack a smile. In fact, I may soon start crying. Because it's not Brian's laughter I want to hear right now; it is Michael's.

I keep myself from crying by going down on him. I cover his huge, rigid cock with my soft, wet mouth and I suck him for all I am worth. He puts his hands through my hair, guiding my head the right way. I reach around his waist and keep my mouth around his dick as it softens because I know how good that feels and because I don't want to ever let him go.

Michael

Oh god, Leo, you looked so hot going down on him, so beautiful stuffing his ass! I thought you were going to be too much for him to take, because we both know you're such a huge guy, but he was able to take it all, and still you had him begging for more! He seems so sweet and he's such a cutie, with those big brown puppy dog eyes and that confident little swagger. You really picked a winner.

Now, aren't you glad I pushed you into his arms?

Leo

"Do you wanna come back to my place?" he asks.

And I want to say no, even though he's fabulous. Because if I go to Brian's place, then we might get into a relationship and then that just proves my husband is really gone, and how do I know he's not secretly waiting for me somewhere in this big city? Maybe the next time I see Michael he won't be an illusion.

I chew on my fingers. Would Michael approve of Brian? Would Michael want me to keep being miserable or would he want me to at least try to reach for happiness?

Finally, I respond, with the same answer I gave Michael the day he asked me if I would take him in sickness and in health: "Yes," I tell Brian. "I do."

BUSTED

Kissa Starling

Lydia pulled on the short, flowered skirt and see-through top. She picked up the nylons but decided against them. Andy would only complain they were too restrictive. The heels she settled on made her taller than her five-foot-three frame. They even elongated her legs just a bit, not that she'd be standing for any period of time. A few sprays of melon body splash to the neck, wrist and belly and she was prepared.

Forty minutes to get to the local Gallery Row mall. Andy expected punctuality and she never disappointed him. Lydia rushed to her new, black Ford Mustang and backed out of the driveway. Her phone rang and she pushed the speaker button. What a great option that had turned out to be.

"Hello?"

"Hey, babe. Where are you?" *Like he doesn't know that I'm on my way.*

"On my way. I'll be there in time. I wouldn't miss one of our *dates.*" She checked the time on the dashboard clock.

"What are you wearing?" *My man is such a perv. No wonder we get along so well.*

"Everything that you requested. Why don't you let me drive and then you can see what I'm wearing in person?" She laughed into the phone but Andy stayed silent. At times she wondered what she was doing with such a serious lover, but then she remembered the way he made her feel when he...

"Lydia. Are you there?"

"Yes, I'm here." She squinted against the glare of the car traveling opposite her.

"Tell me what you're wearing." Lydia swerved to the right to avoid going over the yellow line.

"A short skirt..." *So short that my ass peeks out.*

"No panties, right?"

"Of course not. My black thin silk shirt..."

"No bra, right?" *Why can't I ever finish a sentence?*

"No, Andy, no bra. Listen, I have to drive."

"Don't hang up that phone." Silence. "Tell me about your bush."

"Again, just as you like it. I haven't shaved in weeks." *Ten million men like bare pussy and I get an Indian guy who loves hair!*

"Mmm. I can't wait till you get here. You have me hot already. Now get off of that phone. You shouldn't be talking and driving at the same time."

Just thinking of the night ahead spurred tingles throughout her body. "Really? Well then maybe you shouldn't be calling me. See you soon." Lydia pressed the phone button once more to disconnect. He could be so exasperating but oh how she loved his wicked ways. This time they were meeting at the Gallery Row movie theater. It was kind of raunchy and scary. He'd made a big deal about picking the movie. Like it really mattered what they went to see. They had regular spots all over town where they "played," places that usually gave them space and looked away long enough for them to break the public norm.

At 9:57 Lydia pulled into the parking lot and swerved into a front parking space. Andy stood right outside the main entrance, a cigarette in his hand, gazing at some waitress's butt. Just like him. There wasn't a woman out there he wouldn't flirt with. The young girl bent to grind her cigarette in the flowerpot and turned toward the building. Andy stopped her with a hand on her arm. They were still talking when Lydia approached at 10:00 exactly.

"Hey, hon. This is Cindy. She works at Ruby Tuesdays."

She held out her hand and leaned forward to peck Cindy on the cheek. The waitress stepped back with a surprised look on her face. Lydia did see her peek beneath her blouse before she excused herself. "I have to get back to work. Nice meeting you, Lydia."

Andy grabbed Lydia's hand and led her inside. "Hurry, babe. The movie will be starting. We don't want to be late. Maybe we could invite Cindy to play after work?"

"We don't want to miss out on the back row seats, you mean. And you're right—we may have to grab a bite to eat at Ruby Tuesdays afterward."

The two of them stood in front of the lighted marquee. There were twelve movies playing and most of them started in the next five to ten minutes. She knew he'd pick the one with the half-dressed female on the movie poster. Buttered popcorn smells mingled with that of the cheesy nachos.

"How about *Miz Jasmine Goes to Hollywood?*" Andy asked, trailing the woman's cleavage on the poster with his fingers.

Lydia laughed to herself at the choice. "Sounds good to me. I'm going to the bathroom. I'll meet you at the door to the movie."

Lydia rushed to the bathroom to reapply her lipstick and adjust her clothing. A vent she walked over threw a gust of cool wind right between her legs. *A preview of things to come,* she thought. Women scurried around pushing up their boobs, caking on their makeup and eating mints on the way out.

Andy lingered outside the movie entrance. She sashayed across the carpet walking toward him. He clutched her arm and practically dragged her into the theater as soon as the workers moved out of the way with their brooms and dustpans. "Let's find a seat."

They'd stayed within their preordained rules. It was late at night. They'd chosen an X-rated movie so no small children would be there. And now they would sit in the last row. It wasn't like they wanted to get arrested for their fetish—they just wanted to have a little fun in public.

Andy leaned over to kiss her and Lydia met his lips. The opening credits had just started and already his hand was under her blouse. Her nipples rose and stiffened under his touch. His hand wandered down to the waist of her skirt. "Wait. It's not dark yet," she pleaded.

Lydia squirmed around on the seat, trying to make sure no bare skin touched the fabric. They weren't the first to play like this and they certainly wouldn't be the last. The thought of what might be on the stadium seats made her shudder.

With a grin on his face, Andy shoved his large brown hand down, pinched her pussy lip and came back up. "As you wish, my dear."

A couple walked up and sat right in front of them. The couple nodded hello before they took their seats. Andy smiled in return.

"Just the way you like it," she whispered.

"Just the way we both like it," he whispered back. "Now move closer to me."

Darkness descended upon the theater. Andy pushed his nose against her hair and inhaled. Whispers abounded and then turned into silence. He reached under her shirt and squeezed her left tit. She moaned out loud and the lady in front of them turned around. They quit kissing and put their eyes on the big screen. Before she knew it, Andy's hand rested on her knee. It quickly moved up under her skirt. Lydia spread her legs and shifted around in the restrictive movie seat. His fingers entered her pussy and Lydia gasped. Once again the lady in front of them shifted to see what was going on. Lydia smiled at her and began pumping onto Andy's fingers. *I'm such a slut,* she thought to herself.

"Yeah, babe. Fuck my fingers." The man whirled around just as Andy removed his hand and licked his fingers. "Mmm. Tasty." Andy forged ahead and rammed his hand back up under her skirt. The man in front of them twisted to the left and kissed his wife. Lydia leaned back and scooted her ass forward. Her skirt was flipped up now and her pussy was totally exposed for any and all to look upon.

Another couple, a few aisles over, got up and left. Both of them shook their heads back and forth and turned away from Lydia and Andy. Unfortunately, not everyone was into public displays of affection. They didn't understand how free it made you. It was a special kind of love.

Lydia reached up and fondled her breasts through her thin shirt. She loved manipulating her nipples. The man tapped his wife's shoulder and pointed behind them. She giggled and unbuttoned her shirt. Andy pumped in and out of Lydia's pussy and she moaned frequently. Lydia looked up and saw the couple viewing her wanton ways. That was all it took for her to let loose and orgasm quite loudly. "Ahhh." She pinched her nipples as she came.

The couple smiled and turned back to the movie, hands on one another's crotches. "They probably think we're done, babe. Play with it."

Andy unzipped his pants and let his semihard cock flop out. Lydia took it in her hands and stroked. She stared her lover in the eye and ran her tongue across her lips. "I so want to suck you."

"Don't let me stop you. Suck me, babe."

Lydia let the arm between them up and leaned over into Andy's lap. Her mouth formed a perfect O around the now fully-erect cock. "Mmm." She saw a man a few rows over look at them and give a thumbs-up sign. Andy rocked and shoved his cock deeper and deeper into her mouth. Lydia took every inch and prayed for more. She imagined fixed eyes glaring behind where she now kneeled. If they only knew how an audience flipped her horniness level to infinity and beyond.

His skin tasted citrusy. Her taste buds couldn't get enough of it. She sucked him until he pulled her away, and then went to sit back down. Very rarely did she get to finish him the first time. Andy held her hips and pulled her down onto his lap. She gasped for breath when his cock invaded her slick pussy. He pushed the upper part of her body forward and locked his hands on her hips.

"Oh, yes, babe. Do it."

Her friends classified this as *risky behavior*. Lydia called it fun. She was addicted. There was no way she'd ever be able to give this up. Exhibitionism had become a drug as real as cocaine.

Lydia bent forward, her face inches away from the couple in front of them. They turned in unison to look straight at her, and to share. They were finger-fucking and stroking one another. She wanted to quit, she really did, but his cock felt so fucking good in her warm, tight pussy. There was no way she was giving that up. Watching the other couple turned her on tenfold. Lydia got the fucking of her life while everyone who sat close by watched. She shot directly up when the orgasm hit her. Without thinking, she pressed her palms against her tits and pushed them together in a pinup pose as she came. It was at that exact moment that the screen lit up for an outdoor scene. All eyes were on her.

"Well, I never!" she heard a woman up ahead of them exclaim.

Without thinking Lydia lifted her shirt up to her neck, jutted out her tits, and yelled, "Well maybe you should!"

The woman's companion laughed and she slapped him. They left soon afterward. *Their loss,* she thought. *I couldn't stop if I wanted to.*

Andy shot his spunk into her pussy right when the after-gasms hit her. This forced her into coming over and over again. She only yelled out once but it caused the entire audience to turn this time. She instantly collapsed onto the seat in front of her, with her elbows on the top, and pretended she'd been watching the movie. Andy lifted her up and directed her toward her own seat where she smoothed the front of her skirt and held her hands in her lap. She was now the epitome of a good girl.

How she longed to check up on the fucking progress of the other couple.

Lydia reached over with her left hand and tucked Andy's cock back into his pants. He zipped them up right before the manager and an usher reached them. "Is there a problem here, folks?"

The couple in front of them listened with anticipation. Apparently they'd fumbled enough to look presentable. "No problem here, sir. We're really enjoying the movie. Care to join us?" Andy moved over and patted the seat between the two of them.

"We've had a few complaints about indecent exposure."

"Hmm, now that is a dilemma. I can't imagine who would want to have sex in a movie like this one." Andy said it so convincingly that Lydia almost believed it hadn't been them screwing out in the open.

"I think you should come with us, you two." The stern look on the manager's face left no room for interpretation.

"You didn't want to finish the movie, darling?" Lydia beamed her sweetest smile.

"I was finished, babe. Here, at least. Let's go with these nice gentlemen."

The couple stood up and walked behind the theater staff. They'd never gotten quite this close to getting caught before. Lydia wrung her hands but Andy kept a cool, collected façade for all to see. The manager led them inside his office and shut the door. He picked up the phone and began dialing.

"Now see here, sir. We've done nothing wrong. Do you have proof of these improprieties that you speak of?" Andy's back was straight as a board. He was in lawyer mode.

"I run a family establishment. I can't have you kind of people frequenting my place." The manager set down the phone but he was adamant about his feelings.

"I see. So the teenagers who were smoking pot in the bathroom—that was okay for families to see? The five men on-screen gangbanging the lady—that was a family show? And the video games you have in the lobby. The ones where you kill people for driving in front of you...I guess those are *family oriented*?" Andy's face had turned red. He leaned over the manager's desk and pounded on it.

"I don't want any trouble, sir. You and your lady friend just leave and don't come back."

"Like we'd want to!" Andy grabbed Lydia's hand and they rushed out the door. By the time they'd reached the parking lot they were almost flying. Laughter erupted from both of their guts. "Now we move to the car. I'm going to drive down I-85 where all of those bright lights are." Andy knew no danger.

"Oh, you mean where it seems like it's daylight in the middle of the night?"

"Exactly. You'll suck my cock while I drive. Every trucker from here to the state line will be jealous as hell."

"Whatever you say, darling. I aim to please."

"No, babe, I'll do the aiming and you do the pleasing."

"I will miss drinks with Cindy." Lydia put on her pouting face and looked at Andy, batting her lashes. "But we can meet up with her next weekend. She slipped *me* her number!"

"Exactly why we fit so well, babe."

SATISFACTION GUARANTEED

Sommer Marsden

Jared thought he might lose his mind soon. The pregnancy was almost over, but by god, it felt to him as if she'd been pregnant for years. And then he felt like a shit for feeling that way. After all, it was Sheryl doing all the heavy lifting, so to speak. It was his lovely wife who peed about sixty times a day and who had the indigestion and the insomnia and the kicking. So, being sex starved, tired, scared and thoroughly unsatisfied was ridiculous and borderline cruel.

But he still missed her.

His wife. Them. Together. He missed the morning sex where they avoided kissing because it was just better to use those morning-breath mouths on a nipple or a clit or a cock. He missed yanking her into a hot shower with him afterward. He missed afternoon sex on the days they both worked from home. Seeing her face reflected in his laptop screen as he bent her over the chair behind his makeshift desk in the kitchen. And he missed the night sex, after the movie or before the movie or half asleep. Basically, he missed his wife and her body and her mouth on him. He daydreamed about pushing into her, sliding the length of her wet pussy and not having to reposition her sixty-two times so that it was comfortable. And he was tired of being terrified of hurting the baby, or squishing the baby, or poking the baby in the head with his damn penis.

He was ready for the birth, ready to welcome his son into the world, reclaim the woman he loved, and by god, get laid again eventually. And that made him feel like a heel.

"Hey, there. Where'd you go?" Sheryl asked. She stood, her roundness framed like an art photo, in the archway between dining room and living room.

"Nowhere. Off to Never Never Land, I guess." He grinned and stifled a yawn. Neither of them was getting much sleep it seemed. Sheryl could never get comfortable so she tossed and turned. When she tossed and turned, he woke. And so the circle went. He would lie in the dark and put his hand on her stomach and sometimes kiss her. Just kiss her. But in his mind he did so much more. In reality, he tried to let her rest. Brody would kick his hand and he would wonder how they would be as a family unit when the time came.

"Well, Peter Pan, run up there and get me my fries. Only Jimmy's fries will do." It was Sheryl's turn to yawn but she looked happy; ready to pop and exhausted, but happy nonetheless.

"Right. They should be ready. Be right back." He kissed her belly, kissed her full red lips and out the door he went.

Jimmy's was a hole-in-the-wall diner up the street. Sitting squatly on Main Street, it was a square silver throwback to the days of red vinyl stools and chrome counters. The kitchen was the size of a large closet. He knew because not too long ago he had made extra money working in that stifling cramped kitchen. But then the gig as a full-time reporter had come through and he had been able to say good-bye to the grease in his hair and the burns on his forearms. But not before Sheryl had become fully addicted to the fries.

Jared cut up the back way, through his neighbor Bernie's backyard, over the fence, up the back path past the veterinarian and the old-lady hair salon. He spotted the back door to the diner propped open, hot as the oven it contained. Even though the day was cold enough to show his breath, he knew it was an easy triple digit in the sweatbox where they cooked.

A little closer still and he could make out Dana's long legs. She was tall with a dyed black Bettie Page 'do and legs that must've reached her neck. She wore her fifties-style uniform at all times, whether she was manning the fryer or the booths. Dana took great pride in her bubblegum pink getup and her crisp white apron. The patent leather Mary Janes were just a perk and Jared had no earthly clue how she could stand wearing them for a shift. Then again, she was a girl, and despite marriage, for the most part girls were still a mystery to him.

He was close enough to call out a *Howdy!* but it died in his throat when Chuck came up behind her and pressed the flat of his jeans to the back of her skirt. Chuck and Dana had just purchased Jimmy's. They were only the third owners. The original Jimmy had died ages ago. Tom Streat had sold them the diner about three months back. Chuck shoved his big hands under his wife's skirt and lifted. As she cleaned the counter, he tugged at her pale aqua panties. Definitely not a thong, these were a throwback to the days when dames wore real undergarments. And somehow the bigness of them by today's standards made Jared's cock go hard. Harder than the morning wood that haunted him now that sex was just a pipe dream.

Or maybe, he thought, rubbing his fingers hesitantly up the

rigid length of his hard-on, it was the yards of pale leg that unwound from the leg holes of those panties. Dana had gams, that was for sure, long muscles that were pale like milk. He caught the flash of a brown birthmark at the top of her thigh, part of it hidden under the aqua elastic. He wondered if Chuck ever traced it with his tongue before eating her pussy. Or during. Did he take breaks to tongue her birthmark? With that thought, Jared took a giant step back into the protection of the copse of trees.

Was he really going to do this?

Now it wasn't just his fingers on his dick, it was the whole flat of his palm, warm and already finding a rhythm, though he was still in denial. He was not, not, not going to stand in some trees and watch them fucking around and jack off like some horny teenager. Not.

He told himself that all the way through the moment that Chuck pulled those panties down over the snowy swell of Dana's ass and his hand finally relented and pulled down his zipper.

Jared pressed his back to the tree behind him, praying on some level in his stunned mind that no one would stumble over him until they were done—until he was done. He slid his fist the length of his cock and watched big, ruddy Chuck bend long, lithe Dana over the stainless steel counter. Her elegant hands, one finger twined with a Celtic knot tattoo, wound through the back slats where utensils hung. She spread her legs and the panties stayed frozen right below her knees, barring her from spreading wider. Keeping her tight, he imagined. He fisted his cock faster, wondering when he was ever going to feel a cunt again and pushing away the guilt that came rushing at him on demon's wings.

Chuck positioned himself behind his wife and the time finally occurred to Jared: one thirty, post-lunch peace. The flurry of activity had ceased and now there was a lull. And the couple had every intention of taking advantage.

Cold wind swept past him like a secret spy watching his every perverted move. He expected to lose his erection but then Chuck tapped one round asscheek and then the other with the hard pole of his cock. Dana's amused laughter carried through the air and tickled at his ear even as the warm coil of pleasure seemed to wrap around him at the base of his spine, his cock cold but hard and ready in his hand.

Chuck was in and Jared was envious—of the warmth he knew he felt and the sounds he knew were filling his ears. He could hear them from here, some of them, at least. Little sounds of pleasure and want and need that fluttered up and out of Dana's throat like a siren's song. "Oh, baby. Right there," she said.

"Right there," he echoed, his eyes never leaving them even as his motions became faster, more eager.

Chuck gripped her hips, slammed home; not gentle, not in the least. His wide hand, with russet hair at the knuckles (he knew from when Chuck took his money) snaked around and found the neat trimmed triangle of her bush. His fingertips worked between the folds of her sex and he started circles, faster and faster circles that would be the beginning of the end of her—and himself, Jared realized. Because he could all too well imagine the soft warm flesh under Chuck's fingertips, the internal tightening that gripped her slick warm pussy up around his thrusting cock like a velvet ribbon.

"Oh, yeah." Shit! He clamped his lips together to stifle any other errant thoughts that might want to come shooting out of his mouth. And speaking of shooting, he was done for very, very soon. He had a hair trigger these days.

"Oh, baby. Yes." Dana's voice was louder on the wind. She

was louder. And for just an instant, when her dark head turned his way, Jared swore she was looking at him.

But then he was lost in the urgent thrust and bump of Chuck and the imagined feel of a hot wet cunt around his shaft. He watched how the fingers of the big man's hands bit into the snow white flesh of her hips and the way she arched back and the way her long, black hair shifted and slid over her back like an inky shadow. Her orgasm could probably be heard a few blocks off.

That did him. It reminded him of Sheryl's vociferous approval of their fucking and his own warm come flowed over his hand. For a moment, he closed his eyes to right the world. It seemed to be moving. He soaked up every flicker and rumble of his orgasm and cherished it. He should beat off more, he realized, at least for now, until his little family unit found a rhythm again.

When he opened his eyes, Chuck was buttoning up but Dana was staring at him. Even from this distance, he could see it now. She'd known all along that he'd been out here on the back path. She dropped him a wink and turned back to the fryer.

"Hey there, Jared." Her color was high and her eyes were a bit glassy. Post-orgasm euphoria, he thought. "I dropped another batch in for you. The last ones got cold."

"I...I um, got tied up. Hung up. I mean, sorry!" His tongue seemed to have doubled in size and his heart beat so strongly he expected to drop dead any moment. God. What had gotten into him? But in his mind he could still see her, head thrown back as she came, voice carrying on the slight fall breeze. He shivered and tried to cover with a laugh. "I'm a space cadet these days."

Her big blue eyes found his and she smiled. It was a very kind and sincere smile. "Feel better?"

He wasn't sure what to say at first. So he only nodded, feeling the red-hot stain of mortification on his cheeks. She nodded in a businesslike way that almost made him laugh. "Good. Tell Sheryl I put extra grease in her greasy fries."

He let out a breath he hadn't realized he was holding and nodded. "Got it. Extra greasy grease for my girl and my baby."

"When is she due again?" Her eyes flicked over him and he felt soothed by her gaze. What a bizarre thought. But everything was softened and muzzy from his recent release.

"Any day now. Day after tomorrow, officially." He gathered the brown paper bag with its already migrating grease stain. He was anxious now to be home to his wife.

"Ah, good. So, I hope she enjoys." She nodded to the bag.

"I'm sure she will." Jared turned to go. Back down the path with his offering of craving defeating food.

"Oh, and Jared?"

He turned to see a sly smile spread over her kewpie-doll mouth. "Yeah?"

She gave him her come-hither finger and his stomach bottomed out. Was she going to scold him or threaten to tell Chuck or...his mind went in circles like a rat in a cage. He had to force himself to walk forward in sort of a drunken man shuffle. "Yeah?"

She leaned in and offered a wide array of cleavage and flashes of tats that went on to only Chuck knew where. "I hear that a good way to get her going, you know, to start things off is a little..." She made a swirl with her kitten pink tongue and he felt his dick get hard again. "Clit action. So, why not a snack for her. And one for you. It might get the ball rolling, so to speak, and you can get off and everyone will be happy and..." She nodded to a beat-up old sign over the ancient sandwich bar: SATISFACTION GUARANTEED.

"Everyone will be satisfied."

"Guaranteed." She turned on her Mary Janes and flipped him a wave.

When Sheryl was done with her snack, Jared started his. He held her thighs wide and made her come. It might invite labor, it might not. It didn't matter. And when his new life found its rhythm, he planned on investing in a pair of pale aqua retro panties for his lovely wife. Then he'd peel them off of her and show her how much he had missed her—several times. Satisfaction guaranteed.

ROSSE BUURT

Geneva King

De Wallen is Amsterdam's infamous Red-Light District, or *rosse buurt,* as they say in the native tongue. Working girls—and guys—strut their stuff in windows before an audience of serious customers, and many gawking tourists, the latter trying to decide if they're turned on or bothered by the display. At least, if they're anything like me they are.

In a city as beautiful and scenic as Amsterdam, the Red-Light District is a shock even to those of us expecting it. During the day, Amsterdam is a quaint city. But at night, the *rosse buurt* beckons.

Finding De Wallen is easy enough. I just follow the crowd, some of them men with sheepish looks and upturned collars and expressions that say, *I don't normally do this. Really.* There are women too; we hate to be left out. I, like the rest of them, get the once-over from people wondering what side we're on. Pro or customer? Tourist or activist?

The Dutch make it obvious you've arrived. If the buildings

don't give it away, the artwork will. On one street, I step over a bronze breast. Farther down, I see a statue of a woman selling her body from a doorway.

One side of the crowded street is a sea of lit windows. There must be dozens, all filled with people. For a moment, they look like half-dressed mannequins, but then I see one move, hitting the window to attract passersby.

It's easy to tell the first-time visitors. Their eyes are stuck to the scene; not even the jostling of the crowd can break their rapt attention. Me, I feel like I'm experiencing a million emotions at once. You'd think I'd never seen a prostitute, or even a stripper, but somehow in the *rosse buurt,* in a city where sex is both celebrated and regulated, the girls look different from the tired women I see crowding the corners at home, hurriedly negotiating a fee before vice can shut them down.

A few feet away, a couple points to a window. The girl inside wiggles her hips suggestively and motions for them to come closer. The woman giggles nervously and puts up a hand, her wedding band glinting in the light. "No thanks."

"Are you sure?" her husband asks. He leans close and whispers something in her ear, but his eyes never leave the blonde in the window.

Her eyes narrow as he speaks, while the hooker motions again.

The wife shakes her head. She's serious. No.

The blonde dismisses them and moves on to a more promising customer. The man looks disappointed before he's dragged away by his wife. He catches my eye and shrugs as if to say, *Oh well.* Oh well is right. It's easy to lose your head here if you aren't careful.

All visitors to De Wallen are told three things. One, watch your purse or wallet. The thick crowd is a mecca for pickpockets and thieves. Two, don't buy anything on the street: drugs, whores, pottery, anything. Three, don't take pictures. The girls don't like it.

Apparently, they're serious. There's a big commotion farther along the canal. Two men are arguing, one short but solid, the other quite a bit taller. Everything about the tall one screams ignorant American tourist as he holds the camera out of his opponent's reach. Finally, the short guy, who looks like some kind of guard, gives up and pushes him in the canal. The jerk emerges, water sputtering from both him and the camera. The girls in the window cheer and beat on the windows to show their appreciation and the guard bows.

The women of De Wallen (and I focus on them because the men hold no interest for me, not even the ones that look like girls until closer inspection) are surprisingly diverse. Diverse. It seems odd to be using a word like that here, like I'm in a human resources meeting and not in sex central. Assorted. Varying. Maybe those work better.

Dark flesh tones, deep olive hues, and pale alabaster sprinkle the windows. I'm told not to come when they're illuminated by daylight, it's best to look by the magic of night lights. Darkness covers many a sin, some that both seller and customer might prefer to remain hidden.

A few girls gesture to me as I drift past, but when I politely shake my head, they give up and move on to someone with the inclination to play. I'm not that person.

Until I reach her window.

Up to that moment, I'd been shifting with the crowd, allowing the wave of people to carry me in whatever direction they were moving, but now I stand still and plant my feet firmly to the ground.

She's no Julia Roberts, but she's got an elegance that takes my breath away. She stands in her window on the second story, not banging on the glass like the other girls, just standing, surveying the crowd, like she picks the customer and not the other way around, like she's deciding who is lucky enough to experience any bit of her.

My panties dampen, just a little.

I promptly feel ashamed. While I've had my share of one-time encounters, the thought of buying sex bothers me. To be honest, I probably did pay for it each time: a drink to loosen up the cute girl in the bar, dinner at a nice restaurant; all money out of my pocket and there wasn't even a guaranteed payoff at the end of the evening.

But no, it isn't me, it isn't in me to buy sex from a stranger who's just finished servicing someone else and will be looking for the next john or in my case, jane, before I can find my skirt.

Right. I'm taking one last look at her, to affix her image in my mind, when she looks at me. Not one of those glancing, maybe-she-did-maybe-she-didn't looks: she stares straight at me, and waves, a little finger wave like a queen greeting her subject.

I survey the crowd, just to make sure, but no one else around me is looking in her direction. When I turn back, she smiles and points. *Yes, you.*

I smile back, unsure of what to do next. I don't want to waste her time; it's not like I'm in the market to buy.

She widens her stance, so I get a good look at her body. *You like?* she seems to ask.

I like. I like it a lot. I guess from the tint of her skin that she's from somewhere in the Mediterranean, Italy or Greece or somewhere exotic like that.

She turns around, back facing me, then drops into a deep squat and I get a full view of her curvy hips. Her strong thighs support her as she goes up and down; dancing to a song only she knows the tune to. Her tiny skirt provides little cover; even from where I stand I can see—or maybe just imagine—her lips peeking between her legs.

She glances at me over her shoulder and gestures for me to come up.

I step forward, all thoughts of propriety gone; only the pressing desire to touch and be touched by her.

But then I realize she's not gesturing, she's pointing urgently, behind me. I whirl around to find a thief, his hands dragging money from my pocket.

He tries to run, but I grab him by the wrists. "Get off, you bastard!"

He's got my money in his fingers. He's slippery, but I'm pissed. He's muttering in Dutch, which I don't understand, but it sounds like cursing. *Enough of this.* I stomp hard on his foot. When he yells in surprise and hopefully pain, I snatch the money from his fingers and shove him away.

Asshole. Never mess with a woman on a mission.

Speaking of my mission, I turn back to my intended recipient. But her attention is no longer on me, now she's gesturing to someone off to the side. In horror, I realize she's negotiating with another customer. A balding man is shaking Euros at her.

I feel like kicking and screaming. No! She was supposed to be mine! It's only fair. Girl decides to do something crazy, girl gets to do it, not stupid guy takes opportunity from girl. It's not supposed to work that way, dammit!

But the only thing I can do is pout as I watch them come to some sort of agreement. She waves him upstairs and he eagerly disappears inside the building.

I wonder if this is how the prince felt when he went to visit Rapunzel. Rapunzel, Rapunzel, let down your hair. Only in this case it was *let me in, I have money.*

Before she leaves to meet him, she finds me in the crowd. She shakes her hand at me; I realize she's asking if I got my money. I nod and she claps.

I smile, somewhat grudgingly, but how can I help it? She's too cute to stay mad at.

She sweeps her hand to invite me up—I guess I'm to be the next customer—but the spell is broken. I'm in no mood to follow Bald Guy.

I shake my head regretfully and move on. Wherever the pickpocket is, I hope his foot is throbbing.

My head hurts from the experience of De Wallen, so I head back to the hotel. Somehow I need to process this, try to understand what happened to me down there. I almost paid for an interlude with a prostitute. In the safe walls of my hotel, the word alone makes me shudder.

No more De Wallen. You've seen what you wanted to.

So I stay away from the *rosse buurt* and its hypnotic allure, instead exploring the city with my coworkers. There is plenty to do: museums, tours, festivals. Anyone who thinks New York is the city that doesn't sleep has never been to Amsterdam. Our nightly destination is the Leidseplein; no matter how many times we go there's always something new to discover. I attack the town with the fervor of a tourist, flashing money (I'm on an expense account), drinking wine, and dancing; looking at pretty women, but not touching. My reaction to De Wallen is enough to dampen my ardor. Each night I stumble into bed with mere hours before I have to wake up and pretend to be professional.

On our last night in Amsterdam, I beg off from the group. I need to pack, get organized, be ready to leave at the ungodly hour we're booked for. "Fine," they say, "but if you change your mind, we'll be at the Holland Casino."

For a while, I do as I planned. I lay out my clothes, wrap the gifts I'd bought my mother, and get into my pajamas.

An hour later, I can't stand it anymore. My last night in a beautiful city and here I am wasting it away in bed.

I set out for the Holland Casino. I take one of my last trips down the canal and drink my fill of the elegant buildings.

"Are you liking Amsterdam?" the boat operator asks in broken English.

"Yes, very much. I'd love to come back."

"There is always more to see. And I can take you on a tour, very good tour."

I smile back. "That would be nice."

Suddenly, I'm aware of a red glow sparkling on the water. The Red-Light District. I curse inwardly, all week I'd been avoiding De Wallen, trying to quash the desire to go back. But here, mere feet away, the temptation is too great.

"Stop."

The boy looks startled. "Excuse me?"

"You can..." *Are my palms sweaty?* "You can let me out here."

He shrugs like he sees this all the time. He probably does. "Do you want me to wait for you?"

I'm almost tempted to change my mind, to keep going, but I don't. "No. I'll be fine. Thanks." I pay him and scramble out before my good sense gets the best of me.

On my first trip, I kept pace with the crowd. This time, I feel less like a tourist and more like a regular customer. I get my bearings, then stride through the street, looking for her window (second floor, by the statue), hoping she's there and available. I can't strike out twice.

Did you intend to come here all along?

I push the thought out of my head. And then I see her, standing in her window, just as commanding as she was three days ago, that same discerning look that captivated me before.

This time I don't take any chances. I jump up and wave to get her attention. It works. At first she looks mildly offended, until she recognizes me (or at least I think she does). I pull a few euros from my bra and hold them up. She squints, then waves me to the stairs.

A security guard meets me, pats me down, and gestures for me to follow him. The hallway isn't well lit and I can hear the activity in the rooms as I pass.

When I get to her room, the guard raps on the door. She opens it and lets me in. Once I'm inside, his job is done and he walks away with a grunt.

Her room is simple, most of the space taken up by a plush bed. I try not to think about how many people have lain in that bed, how many people have done her in that bed.

Maybe this was a bad idea. I'm starting to feel queasy.

As if she senses this, she leads me to the bed and rubs my shoulders as I try to catch my breath.

"Sorry," I say, hoping she understands English. "It's my first time."

She nods, which reminds me, this is business for her. She's not interested in my personal crises.

"How much?"

This she clearly understands. "Fifty euro, suck." She gently brushes my pelvis, sending a flame of pure lust through my body. "Seventy-five euro, fuck."

She gets up from the bed, searching through a box on the shelf until she finds a dildo in a harness. She hands it to me for my approval.

It's thick. I'm not used to dicks, don't use them much in my real life, but then again, this isn't real life. "Okay. Yes."

"Yes?" She grins. One of her teeth is slightly crooked, but on her it looks endearing. "Me? You?"

The hard rubber fills my hand as I squeeze it. "I'll wear it."

I'm not sure of the protocol. Get undressed or wait for her lead? Pay now or later? I lay the money on the dresser. She nods and starts to pull my clothes off. I lie down on the bed to watch her shed her skimpy outfit. She knows how to put on a show, teasing her breasts with the silk bra until they tumble out of their confines, revealing dark nipples. Real, I'm pleased to see, nothing fake about her. She inches her panties down, past her hips and thick thighs until curly hairs peep through. I realize I'm holding my breath and slowly let it out, afraid I'll wake up and find it's all a dream.

All too soon, it's over and she's kneeling between my legs and her tongue is curling under my clit and she's coaxing the orgasm from my body, which is both compliant and resistant at once.

When I finally come, it feels like it's ripped from me. My cunt clenches around her fingers, still quivering under the force of the orgasm.

She looks pleased with herself, with a cocky self-assured smile on her lips as she pulls me to my feet. Even though my legs are still shaking, I manage to get into the harness to let her adjust it.

"Good?"

"Good." I'd never understood the appeal of the strap-on; it always seemed like an elaborate game of pretend, but now that one is fixed tightly around me, it suddenly becomes clear.

And I know how I want her.

I pull out a chair and sit down, so my dick (yes, *my* dick) points up toward the ceiling. "Come here."

Before she can sit, I push her legs apart. "May I?" I asked, gesturing so there's no doubt what I want.

She nods and I feel for her lips, caressing her pussy until my fingers move easily in her moisture, until her breath quickens and her legs buckle.

Then I let her straddle me, watching as her cunt swallows the dildo and our pubic hair mashes together. Her heavy breasts swing in my face and I capture a nipple between my teeth, sucking the flesh deep into my mouth. My hands knead her ass, the soft cheeks that mesmerized me the first night I saw her, before the thief ruined my moment. But I'm here with her now, tasting her, buried deep inside her, and all my reservations have disappeared and the only thing I'm feeling is euphoria as I head for orgasm number two.

She's slamming onto my thighs, hard. All I can do is hold on as she hurtles toward her climax.

She comes, and for a split second, I focus on her, her face scrunched up in pleasure, until the sensation rolls over me and we're wrapped together, hearts pounding as we try to catch our breath.

Awkwardness quickly sets in. I already paid; do I need to say something? Is "Good job" customary? Do people normally talk or hug or do you just get ushered out as she goes to look for her next client?

She rubs her eyes and yawns. Suddenly I'm exhausted, but I have the luxury of going back to my warm bed before passing out on a plane. She'll be up for hours more.

I slide another wad of Euros on the counter. "So you can sleep." I mimic the motion so she knows what I'm talking about.

"Dank U wel." She rubs my cheek and walks me to the door. The guard meets me and walks me down the hall and out into the warm Amsterdam night.

At the canal, the boat operator is still there. When he sees me, he sails over.

"Have fun?" he asks.

He doesn't know the half of it. "Yes, I did."

He leaves me to my thoughts until we reach my hotel and he helps me out. "I hope you come back."

I think of that second-story window by the statue and the lovely occupant whom I hope is sleeping peacefully. Smiling, I tip him generously. "You know, I think I will."

I'VE ONLY GOT EYES FOR YOU

Rachel Kramer Bussel

There are some things you can only do with the person you've committed your life to, at least, that's been the case for me. Some of my friends take the opposite approach; they were wild and slutty in their single days, having threesomes, going to orgies, being kinky, but since they've gotten married, they're all straight as an arrow. Doggy-style is about as risqué as it gets in their houses, and their husbands have to beg for a blow job.

I've never been that way with Troy. I fucked him on our first date and have always been open about just what kind of woman I really am. I like to watch porn, I find women just as attractive as men, I get wet when I give a blow job. I could go on, but you get the idea: I like sex, plain and simple; with him, with other people. We sometimes go to our local sex club, where we may swap partners, but the best part of anything we do, for me anyway, is watching my hunky husband in action. He's pushing forty but looks about a decade younger. He works out diligently and has a strong, rippling chest, powerful legs, big strong arms and, yes, a nine-inch cock that keeps going and going. No wonder so many other women (not to mention a few men) want to fuck him.

We are a perfect team, because we both have a very high sex drive. That's what initially attracted us to one another, but I agreed to marry him because he is so much more than just a man who can make me come. He makes me breakfast every morning, checks in on me when I'm at home and he's at the office, plans fabulous vacations, and just knows me better than I know myself in many ways. In turn, that lets me relax around him; I never feel like I have to be on guard or watch what I say. With past lovers, as wild as I might have been, I'd get home and worry that they liked me in bed, but only in bed. I would second-guess some of the dirty thoughts that made their way out of my brain and into our naughty talk. With Troy, I know he loves me not in spite of my wild ways, but because of them.

That's how we wound up making our foray into amateur porn. He saw an ad that said we could win a thousand dollars by entering a video of ourselves fucking in this contest. First, let me make it clear that it wasn't about the money. We live in a huge house in one of the finest suburbs of Houston. We are plenty well-off and if we needed to raise money in a hurry, I doubt it would be through porn. But the way his face lit up, I knew he really wanted to do it, and the more I thought about it, the more I did, too. We'd bought a video camera the year before, when we'd been talking about me getting pregnant. So far that hadn't happened, but aside from one time he filmed me sucking his cock and another time we tried taping ourselves fucking but got the angle all wrong, we hadn't really used the camera for much.

We started by researching what was out there, but often wound up collapsing into fits of giggles. A lot of the stuff we watched either looked too slickly produced to truly be "amateur," or it was so amateur that it had lost all its hotness factor. "I want every guy who watches this to want to fuck you," Troy told me, then pulled my face close for a kiss. I shivered as his tongue slipped into my mouth, as dominant and possessive and powerful as it had been six years ago on that date, when he'd kissed me like that on my doorstep, then made me wait the rest of the night for another kiss. He has a big mouth, one that can easily overwhelm my delicate one, and I love it when he practically fucks mine with his tongue. He tickled the top of my mouth, then sucked on my bottom lip hard. I whimpered and my pussy started to ache in that special way that only Troy can make it do. Yes, we sometimes swing or invite people to join us, but only Troy knows exactly how to get me so wet all I want is his oversized cock pounding away at me. I turned over onto my stomach and he pushed up my skirt, then simply stared at my white mesh panties, which I knew barely obscured my pussy, especially when it was so wet. I put my head down on the bed, my arms above my head, and waited for him.

"Oh, Lindsey," he moaned as he peeled down my panties just enough to reveal my sex. "I have to go get that camera. I want to show everyone how wet you are. I hope even that boss of yours sees this: how I make you come, how wild you get when you're horny." He leaned down and nuzzled my pussy with his tongue, licking me tenderly until my fingers curled around the sheets, before getting up and going to the closet for the camera. I'd been all for the idea, but all of a sudden, my face went hot.

When he came back and tried to film me gazing up at the camera adoringly, I put my hand over my face. "This is my wife, Lindsey. Seems she's a little shy, though I have no idea why. Look at that beautiful body, all that glossy brown hair, and that ass. Don't you just want to spank it?" he asked, and then did just that. He must've been holding the camera in one hand and spanking me with the other. He tugged my panties up so they pressed into my pussy. It could've hurt, if it didn't feel so damn good. "This is what she looks like when she really needs to be fucked. She'll do anything I tell her to when she's in that state. Won't you, baby?" he asked me.

"Mmm-hmm," I mumbled in reply.

"Turn over, Lindsey," he said, and I did, squinting up into the camera, part of me wanting it to see me, all of me, and part of me just wanting Troy to fuck me already. "Take off your top, and then your panties. Everyone wants to see your tits and your pussy." For a moment, I pictured our favorite local bar pausing the evening news in order to pop in this tape, starring the girl who drinks Miller Light, about to get fucked by her husband. It made me blush even harder, my thin tank top getting tangled above my head for a second before I freed myself. Then the panties: they were already partway down my legs, so I sat up and then pulled them off, glad I'd gotten my pussy waxed at my regular appointment a few days before. My panties were wet and sticky, as was to be expected.

"Hold up those panties. Give our viewers a really good look," he told me, and I opened them up so "they" could see my juices clinging to the fabric. Now I was getting even more embarrassed, but it was hot, too. I like it when Troy tells me what to do, and I've never not followed his orders. In fact, the more they make me uncomfortable, the hotter they make me, so the next one was tailor-made for me. "Now put the panties in your mouth. Ball them up and shove them right in, unless you want me to do it." Oh god. Was he really going to make me do this? I don't mind people knowing what I look like naked, but knowing how turned on I got by being degraded like this, by being ordered into depravity by my husband, was another thing.

Who would see this? What would they think of me? Would guys sit and watch with their cocks in their hands, jerking off onto the screen—on me?

I took the panties and rolled them up as best I could, then stuffed them in my mouth. "Very good, Lindsey," Troy said. It reminded me of the way he talks to his driving students, patiently guiding them even when they're about to head off the road. But with me, it's different, always has been. Underneath the calm veneer is a man who gets off on telling me what to do. I could see how hard his dick was already. "Now spread those pretty legs for me," he told me, and for him, I did. I let him film my pussy, I even held my toes with my hands to stretch myself as wide open as possible.

Troy then shut the camera off for a minute, got out the tripod that we bought at the same time, but had never used, and mounted it by the end of our bed, so it'd capture as much of our fucking as possible. "Get on top," he told me. "I want to suck on your nipples."

By now, I was so wet, I'd do anything for him. Plus he wasn't just sucking on my nipples. He bit them, bit them in a way that was at once gentle and painful, his teeth sinking in bit by bit, and then keeping going. He took one and looked right at the camera as he held that same breast with his hand and started to pull my nipple away from my body with his teeth. At first, it felt good, sending zaps of excitement to my pussy. But then it started to hurt. I couldn't breathe through my mouth so I breathed as much as I could through my nose. He kept tugging, his teeth deep into my nipple by then. Part of me wanted him to stop, and part of me wanted him to do the same thing to my other nipple. I've never let another man go so far with my body, but for Troy, I've worn nipple clamps on a road trip, I've gotten my clit pierced, I've gotten an enema, I've let him come all over my face. It's not about wanting to be a good wife; well, not entirely. For me, it's more about letting him show me what I can take, what I can learn to like.

I smiled as best a woman with her own panties stuffed in her mouth can, letting the camera, the viewers, know how much he turned me on. "Okay, we can take those out," Troy said. "I want them to hear you scream."

I blushed again because I do tend to scream, loudly, so loudly that hotel security has been summoned to our various rooms on more than one occasion, and I've had to peep out the door with my hair disheveled and face flushed and know that the man standing before me is picturing me getting hammered in the most depraved way possible. "What do you want, Lindsey?" Troy asked me.

He knew exactly what I wanted, but he wanted to hear me say it. "I want your cock. I want it all the way down my throat," I told him, then started to suck his cock, so hard and ripe and ready for me. I couldn't imagine any woman watching this would see it and not want to suck it.

He let me go down on him for a few minutes before easing me off. "I think you need a little spanking first," he said.

I smiled, because I always want a spanking from him. He had me lie across his lap, so I could feel his erection pressing up against me. He tilted me toward the camera to show off my ass. Then he brought his hand down hard on my right cheek, followed by my left. "What a pretty handprint," he said, while I just buried my face in my arms. Soon he was breathing heavily as he put his all into making my ass a bright red, into making it jiggle so that my pussy got involved too. He squeezed my ass and then picked up a paddle we keep on our bedside table. The sound rang out in the room and the spanking took on an intensity his hand-spanking had only hinted at. I kept spreading my legs without even noticing it, silently begging him to hit me there, too.

"Get on your hands and knees," he told me when he'd had his fun with my ass. He made me position myself so my pussy was right in front of the camera. That's when it really hit me that we were making porn, that someone would be able to fast forward to just that moment when the only thing on the screen was my pink, wet, glistening cunt, there for the taking. "Lindsey likes to have her pussy spanked, too. I wish I could invite you over to get the chance to smack her right here, but I'll have to show you how it's done." Then he hit me flush on my pussy lips. It wasn't a surprise, and I arched my ass higher, wanting more. But it's one of those things that I don't usually let people know about. I might tell my closest girlfriends I'm into being spanked. They're pretty open-minded, and a few of them are into some wild things, too, but this upped the ante; this was something else. The sound of Troy spanking my sex filled the room, and soon so did my whimpers. Then he ran his fingers along my slit and said, "See? That's how you know she's really wet, that she's really ready for my cock. My wife is a horny bitch, but she really goes wild when I give her a good spanking." Having him talk about me in the third person, to a potential audience of...anyone and everyone, made me bury my face deeper into the sheets.

He decided we were gonna do it doggy-style. "I want them to hear you scream," he whispered in my ear. It occurred to me that this position might not be the most advantageous for our viewing audience, but I didn't really care anymore. I shifted around so the camera could see the length of my body, and Troy got behind me, rubbing his cock against the entrance to my pussy. I tried to push back against him but he held my hips in place. He knows just how to tease me. I turned my head toward the camera and hoped it saw everything I felt for Troy, not just how wet my pussy got. I hoped it knew that he is the only man who could ever get me to do this, the only man I trust enough to be the best slut I can be, because I know he'll still respect me in the morning. Then, without a word, he was plunging his cock deep inside me. "Yeah," I moaned, as he overtook me. My G-spot quickly came to life, and as his balls hit my pussy, I rocked backward against him, enhancing each thrust. He pulled my buttcheeks apart, and I knew my husband was watching his cock go in and out, in and out. I know the sight mesmerizes him, and I squeezed him now with my inner muscles to let him know I was as into this as he was.

The room was mostly silent save for some grunts and yells. We sped up and slowed down, we got into a rhythm, and when he reached beneath me to play with my clit, I started to come, my liquid spilling out of my pussy, my entire being feeling like he had overtaken me, pushed himself in me and right out the other side. When it's like this, when we're on, when the sexual magic manages to flow so perfectly that I hardly know who's who or what's what, only that I'm his, forever and always, I could weep with joy. Instead, I screamed as his cockhead delivered an urgent message to me via the ridged walls of my pussy, telling me to keep on coming. So I did; I came again, and again after that, until I barely knew how many times it'd been, just that I was so open, so needy.

"I want you to taste yourself on me," he said as he pulled out. He made sure the camera saw his wet cock, the one that'd just been inside me. Then he pulled me down the bed, so my legs dangled off its edges, as he fed me his pussy-flavored dick. We both turned slightly toward the camera

Because I know you want to know—yes, we took first place in the contest. The company asked if we want to make another video, this time with the couple who got second place, and now they have us splashed all over their homepage. They even sent a little trophy that Troy put up on our bedroom dresser. "But baby, I want you to know that no matter how many people are watching us, or what we do with anyone else, I only have eyes for you." And that's why I love him even more now than on our wedding day.

"Me, too," I told him, before we turned off the camera and settled into bed for a few hours of doing what we do best.

CALENDAR GIRL

Angela Caperton

Desi Palladino couldn't take her eyes off April, 1958.

The calendar hung on the wall of Stu Gilbert's tiny office at the back of the garage, where Desi brought him coffee and helped keep the books. There were calendars in the garage too, most of them with drawn or painted girls, prettier than any real woman could ever be, but the calendar on the wall of Stu's office was the only one with photographs of real girls, one for each month of the year.

"Whatcha lookin' at, Desi?" Stu bustled through the open door, wiping his hands on a greasy rag. Stu Gilbert was pushing fifty, stocky, almost bald, but he smiled like a naughty twelve-year-old.

Desi's cheeks burned. "Nothing," she mumbled. "Checking the delivery date for the parts you ordered last week."

Stu chuckled. "She's somethin', ain't she?" he sighed and brushed his fingers over April's bare stomach.

"I thought it was against the law to show...I mean..." Desi's mouth turned desert dry.

"I figure somebody screwed up," Stu said.

Miss April's ash blonde hair framed a plump face with ivory skin and pouty lips. Desi wished she had hair that color and the complexion to go with it. Her own hair fell in heavy black waves where it refused to curl over shoulders of pale olive, the gift of her father's Sicilian blood. The calendar girl's breasts curved in gentle slopes, pink tipped and perfect, and her torso, where Stu's finger twitched wistfully, looked firm, with just a hint of flesh around her stomach, then flattened down to a triangle of pale curls with the shadow of a line at its center.

"I have to go, Stu," Desi said, rising to ease past him and the scent of gasoline and tobacco he carried. He laughed as she reached the door.

"If it bothers you, kid," he chuckled, "I can skip to May."

But he didn't take April down, and every day, all month long, Desi worked two or three hours in Stu's office, looking at the girl on the calendar, her mind turning over and over as she thought of the real person, the girl in that picture, somewhere. *She looks so happy. No, more than happy,* Desi thought. *She looks joyous.*

At the front of the calendar, Desi read the address where it was printed, on Stafford Street in San Francisco.

Somewhere out in California, a pretty blonde girl had stripped herself bare before a man, as open to him as a bride to her husband, sinful and brave and so very beautiful, and he had caught her exuberant beauty with his camera. Desi thought about her constantly, trying to imagine what April's life must be like, how she had been caught in that moment, wondering if she had really been as happy as she looked.

Stu didn't mention the calendar again, not directly, but she saw his eyes when he looked at April and heard the catch in his breath. No man had ever breathed for Desi like that, though plenty of them had tried to get their hands in her blouse. Some days, just walking through the garage could be a gauntlet. Desi never, not for a single second of every working day, forgot she was the only antelope in a plain of lions.

For the most part, the guys in the shop weren't slobs or creeps. She might have dated Bobby Dridger or Jeff Culhane if they'd asked her properly, but they were the nice boys who always changed into clean shirts at the end of a greasy day and were too shy even to flirt.

On the morning of May 1, 1958, Desi clocked in early and carefully removed April from the calendar above Stu's desk, revealing May, a redhead as beautiful as April, but far less alluring. Desi carefully placed April in an envelope and hid her on a shelf between two ledgers.

Of course Stu's first words when he arrived were, "Where's April?"

Desi pretended she didn't hear him and Stu, god bless him, didn't ask her again.

All through that spring, sometimes when she was alone in her room at home, Desi stripped her clothes off and imagined posing. She would have died if Mom or Dad had ever caught her at it. She'd not been seen naked by either of them since she was six. Even her doctor had only seen her bra-covered chest.

Only the girls in her high school gym class had seen Desi naked. Desi remembered her terror but also the excitement as she rushed through the shower, hardly daring to look at the other girls, hoping for invisibility, but also realizing many of the other girls raced just as she did. Her gaze trembled and darted on the others to see if they looked at her. She felt embarrassment at being seen, like Adam and Eve ashamed of their nakedness.

Now, Desi wondered if Adam and Eve had been excited as well as ashamed.

Sizing herself up in her mirror, Desi thought she compared favorably to April. Her breasts were bigger, with little dark nipples instead of pink points, and her waist was tight and curved, sexily, she thought, above the swell of her hips. From the back, her bottom was high and firm, rounded and symmetrical as a perfect olive, golden where the sun had never touched her. But what held her eye and tempted her fingers was the patch of silky fur that covered her treasure—Mom's name for her pussy.

A real girl, Desi thought, and slipped her fingers through the satiny moss, but a goddess too, sacred to men, naked and made to be worshipped.

Sometimes she stopped but other days, the thoughts were too much and she reached deeper, across the rough, sweet spot into the heat of her treasure, wet, sometimes dripping, desperate for a touch, or, even better, to be seen.

Closing her eyes before the fire burned her alive, Desi sometimes imagined the girl in the mirror was April.

Desi usually arrived at the shop before anyone else. Stu trusted her with the books—she kept them better than he did. She took calls, handled the payroll, made coffee, and chatted with customers. Some days were slow, especially in the morning. During lulls she would wander to the shelf and draw the envelope from between the two ledgers where she had hidden it, slip it open with nervous fingers and stare, growing wet under her cotton panties.

One Tuesday in late May, she had just put the envelope back between the ledgers and turned toward the doorway, when she turned to see Bobby Dridger standing not two feet behind her and her ragged breath lodged in her chest.

"She's really pretty, ain't she?"

Bobby looked a little like Buddy Holly with muscles. He had tawny, straight hair that he combed back in a wave and he wore black-framed glasses.

His question vibrated the air between them a long time before Desi nodded.

Bobby reached past her and took the envelope from its hiding place. Smiling, he shook April out and held her. April stared up at them, open, no secrets among the three of them.

Heat rolled off Bobby like the purr of a lion in Africa. He smelled like musk and gasoline.

"This is good stuff. It's the light makes the difference." He drew a line with his grease-stained finger, not quite touching the photo, along the curve of April's breast and Desi saw what he meant, the light emerging under Bobby's black, ragged nail.

He looked at Desi, and then back at the picture and lightly touched it, right in the middle of April's treasure. "Somebody missed this," he said, much as he might have pronounced a carburetor dead. "They ought to've airbrushed this."

"What's airbrushed?" Desi asked in a whisper.

"It's a retouch they do on these girls," he said, clearly pleased she had asked the question. "It's why none of them other girls have p... why they don't show hair down there. Come here." The small office shrank to a tiny matchbox. She only took two steps before she stopped, her breast almost touching Bobby's arm. She breathed his breath when he turned and smiled and ran his finger down May's belly, the dark half-moon of his nail skirting the top of the smooth, hairless labia. "See?"

Bobby held April out and grinned. Desi took the page from him, her cheeks burning.

"Desi," Bobby said, nervous, and hopeful. "I sure would like to take your picture."

* * *

"Just sit still, Desi. Relax." Bobby lifted her chin and brushed a wisp of hair from her dark mane so it hung to her eyebrow. She wore a crisp white shirt and a navy blue skirt. He shot against a background of azaleas, their blooms thin and pale at the season's end.

Bright in a clear sky, the sun had just begun to gather shadows as it settled over the town. Bobby said it gave her an aura. In his yellow linen shirt and black chinos, he looked like a college boy.

"Put your arm up behind your hair, baby. Look just to my right." He stepped behind the tripod, snapping several shots as she raised her arm, aware that it made her breasts stand out against the white shirt. The straps and lace of her bra must show, she thought. *What if I wasn't wearing a bra?* Her nipples stiffened.

"Perfect, Desi. Don't even breathe, baby."

The sun's light kissed along the edge of her cheek and the nape of her neck, and pulsed between her legs. Disobedient, she turned her head the tiniest bit and smiled at Bobby, hoping her eyes and the flush she felt in her cheeks conveyed how much she wanted him.

He looked a long moment, then disappeared behind the shutter with a steady *click, click, click.*

When he showed her the pictures the next day, Desi stared at the girl painted in vivid colors, hardly believing it was her.

"Baby, you're amazing," Bobby said. "There's a dozen shots in here I could sell."

She leafed through the pictures. "Who'd buy them?" she asked as her treasure hummed.

"I don't know. Glamour mags? *Popular Photography?* You're a natural, baby. The light loves you."

She thought about April, out in California.

"Desi," Bobby rubbed his chin. "You know what a camera club is?"

She shook her head.

"Like it sounds. A bunch of shutterbugs who get together every few weeks. We share lights and lenses and we pool our dough for a model and sometimes a studio."

"So?" she started, and then she felt herself blush as she understood what he was asking.

Bobby picked her up at ten Saturday morning. She'd done as he said, and wore pretty clothes: a calf-length, pleated red skirt and a pale pink linen blouse, nearly white and nearly sheer. Beneath the blouse, she wore a slivery-gray camisole and beneath that her lightest-weight white bra. Her mother hounded her to wear girdles, but Desi liked her full hips so she left the girdle at home, opting for plain white cotton panties and a garter belt the same color as the camisole. She settled on dark red lipstick and subtle lashes, and, at the last minute, she rolled on her darkest stockings, real silk in rich, charcoal gray.

"It's ten bucks an hour up front," Bobby told her. "But then, if the guys like you, they tip you. There's no funny stuff, baby. These guys are serious. They ain't creeps."

"It's very exciting," Desi answered, feeling a little awkward and foolish, so nervous her treasure had almost soaked her panties.

"Today's shoot is at Ike Bentley's place, which is cool. Bentley's got cash. He has a permanent studio and when we use it, sometimes he springs for costumes and props. I told him about you so this ought to be fun."

Mr. Bentley's house sat on a big lot with a view of Lee's Lake. A young man with a trim moustache answered the door and grinned at Bobby.

"Hey, Charlie, this is Desi," Bobby said as he patted the man on the shoulder.

"I figured." Charlie took her hand into his warm, muscular one and shook it lightly. "You're even prettier than Bobby said." He held her hand a little longer and looked her over with what she guessed was a photographer's eye.

She walked down a parquet hall to a sun-flooded room with a ceiling mostly of glass. Along one side of the big room, she glimpsed richly colored curtains, furniture, and tall flood lamps, but Charlie steered her to the men on the other side. Four of them waited among a forest of tripods.

Bobby made the introductions. Mr. Bentley, handsome for a man of his years; Gus, older too, and quiet, but he had a nice smile. Doug Spencer, dark-eyed and lean; Desi remembered him from his tenure at the garage the summer before. Wetness began to seep between her legs. Before she could squirm, Bobby introduced her to Dr. Barlow. Dr. Barlow, the most eligible young man in town—in spite of his wedding ring.

There were six men, some strangers, others familiar. She smiled at them, feeling the light in her eyes, the shine in her lips, the look she had seen on the beautiful girl in Bobby's pictures. She held the tether of allure for a long moment until Mr. Bentley said, "Perhaps we should get started."

Bentley barked directions, and Charlie moved lights and props and opened shutters and curtains. She wondered if Charlie was like a butler. A look around the room told her that Mr. Bentley might be that rich.

"We'll start over here." Bobby took her lightly by the arm. Her sensitive skin, suddenly thin enough to tear, burned beneath his fingers. He led her to a white wooden chair by a table where a bowl bloomed with roses. "Sit down," he said.

Charlie adjusted the window shutters and Desi blinked

against the wash of golden sunlight.

"Now, just do what they tell you," Bobby said with a wink and stepped behind his camera.

The room rustled and clanked as the tripod forest moved. The intensity of the men's concentration as they adjusted knobs, focused, changed lenses and filters, added to the warm butterflies fluttering in her core.

What would they tell her to do?

"Get her the roses first," Mr. Bentley said and Charlie picked her a bouquet from the bowl, eight perfect red roses that he presented with a bow and a grin.

"Hold them just at your breast and inhale them," Mr. Bentley ordered.

She did exactly as he said, gathering the silky flowers against her pale blouse, breathing them, the sweetness a cloud in the morning, her vision misty against the white windows and the shapes of the men in the light. She smiled, full-breathed, and her breasts pushed out in sharp peaks.

Click, click went the cameras and after a while, she exhaled, though air still felt shallow in her chest, a thin pool where her pounding heart swam.

"All right," Bentley said. "Unbutton the top three buttons of your blouse."

"Yes, sir," Desi said, trying to find Bobby in the glare. She laid the roses in her lap and smiled at the cameras, her fingers at the buttons.

Click, click.

"Hmm," Mr. Bentley said, and Desi hated the note of disapproval she heard in his voice. "That's not going to work as long as you're wearing a brassiere. Do you mind removing it?" He pointed to a changing screen near the colorful furnishings on the other side of the room.

Charlie appeared like a genie to take the roses and she stood and walked to the screen, her breath faster and the line between her legs sodden and dripping. Desi paused beside the screen, looking at the lurid curtains and the sofa, like something in a sultan's harem. She thought of the Arabian Nights and the woman who kept herself alive by telling stories, by enchanting a man with her talents.

She thought of April and her nipples tightened.

She shed her blouse, camisole and bra without hesitation, and before she put the blouse back on, she looked at the costumes on hangers behind the screen. Some of the shining fantasies were no bigger than her hand, and her nipples grew as hard as marbles as she imagined herself in glossy black and white, shining patches of satin. She stole a glimpse of herself in the mirror, unable to look directly at her image, the rising curves with dark rigid tips, and her face that of the woman in Bobby's photos.

She slipped on the sheer blouse and buttoned it to the place Mr. Bentley had asked for, aware of every place the linen touched her, its cling no more than mist, but intense as a warm finger. She stepped from behind the screen, her blood pulsing in her ears, her throat, and her treasure. Almost giddy, she walked toward the men and their cameras.

As she approached the chair, she understood at once that everything had changed. She smelled something in the room, a scent, sharp and tangy, exhilarating and new. She heard their breath, as ragged as her own, but with a primal edge.

Every one of them watched the bounce of her breasts.

She sat and gathered the roses, leaned forward so that the revealed cream of her chest emerged from the linen, her dark nipples harder yet in clinging, translucent pink, her lips parted in a smile, a promise.

The clicking almost deafened her.

"You are everything Bobby said, my dear." Mr. Bentley took

the roses from her this time. He put his hands lightly on her shoulders and his fingertips kneaded her through the blouse. He held her gaze, the unspoken question as clear as a shout. She answered it with a nod. He knelt, his gray eyes intense on hers, not looking down to where his fingers worked at the last four buttons, not until he had finished and stood up so that she could open the blouse and drop it in a whisper to the floor.

Click.

She picked up the roses, spread them in a fan over her breasts, not covering herself at all, letting the red flowers brush the most sensitive spots just below the nipples. The men watched her, rapt, their cameras silent.

She grew still in the moment, the pulse in her treasure and the blazing heat just under her skin, demanding obedience.

She saw the intense shapes against the rising light of the morning sun and tried to find Bobby among them. *Paint me,* she thought to him. *Paint me with light.*

Raising a finger to her lips, she wet it to dripping, then touched her right nipple, slick and shining, catching the sun like the sweat of its luminescent desire.

Gus groaned. *Click, click.*

"Wait," Bobby said, stepping between her and the cameras. She became a goddess under his gaze and his hands felt divine where he touched her shoulders while he turned her slightly in the chair, so that her breast stood in sharp silhouette. He took the roses and selected one, the darkest of the dozen, and rested the cool bloom against her nipple. "Hold it there," he said. Bentley nodded his approval as Bobby stepped back.

She imagined each of the men in turn as an absent lover whose memory had come upon her like a ghost, wistful, vulnerable, the red flesh of the rose the spirit of distant lips, kissing the brown tip of her breast.

"Beautiful," Bentley breathed.

Hundreds of clicks filled the room. They shot her with the roses, without the roses, standing, sitting, her body arched into the light. Her nipples softened only to harden again as Bentley or Bobby posed her, and she felt their arousal as each new seduction unfolded.

Somewhat to Desi's disappointment, no one asked her to remove her skirt.

"We're losing the morning light," Doug Spencer said after a while.

"Time to move to the seraglio," Mr. Bentley laughed. "Would you like some wine or a drink, Desi?"

She picked up her blouse and draped it around her shoulders, a thin vein of self-consciousness creeping into her when the cameras no longer courted their queen. She was glad, but also a little sorry, when Charlie brought her a robe. Smiling, still slick between her legs, her voice trembled slightly as she nodded to Mr. Bentley. "A little wine, maybe?"

Most of the men had a Collins, though Mr. Bentley took straight scotch. They talked about the photos, about film and lenses, things Desi knew nothing about, but they talked to her too, including her in their discussion of the poses, what they saw through their lenses, what they hoped to capture. Her. She. Light made solid on glossy paper for unknown—and known—eyes to see. She sat among them, her breasts still, for all purposes, bare, their gazes easier on her now, though she still saw the heat in their eyes, the anticipation of whatever lay ahead, and she shared that anticipation with them, loving the threads of communion and impulse.

The wine was sweet and barely chilled. Desi had only had wine a few times, at weddings and parties, but she remembered how much she liked it, how the warmth moved under her skin.

When the drinks had been mostly consumed, Charlie helped everyone move their tripods and gear across the room to the Oriental divan at the center of the bank of lamps.

"We'll spend the rest of the afternoon here, Desi," Mr. Bentley said. "I bet you have a good imagination. Our theme will be a night in a harem. Is that all right with you?"

"Sure," she smiled.

"Good. You will want to undress completely. We want all the costumes to look authentic. Are you ready?"

"What should I wear first?" she asked as she started toward the screen. Her head spun a little with the wine and the heat that had collected between her legs.

"Any of the costumes you wish."

Behind the screen, she dropped the robe and her nipples stiffened instantly. She examined the costumes and picked one with a short red jacket and a pair of ballooning ebon pants. She grinned as her hands unfastened her skirt and dropped it beside the robe, unsnapped the garter, and rolled the stockings down her shapely legs.

She felt them on the other side of the screen, six men, all waiting for her. She slid her soaked white panties down her legs. All through the morning, while the men had been shooting her, she'd watched them and felt their desire, saw their erections—some more than others. She knew what men had between their legs—she had seen statues and paintings—but this was different. Statues and paintings were tastefully flaccid, not stiff enough to snap a photo.

As she'd posed for these men, they had all grown hard watching her, wanting her, just as she needed them to see her and to want her. Never, even in her imagination, had anything felt so good, so purely ecstatic.

She peeled away the wet panties and reveled for a moment in

anticipation of their worship, and then she pulled on the harem pants and slipped on the halter that might as well have been made of spun glass.

When she stepped in front of them, the wine's heat spread all through her legs and up her spine. Pleasure she had known in dreams, and a few times when she had touched herself, manifested magically before them, before the wide eyes of lenses.

They posed her on the divan, chastely at first, but then more wantonly, sprawled in opiate abandon, her jacket open and then gone altogether.

"Change," Mr. Bentley commanded and she obeyed, wearing a bra made of golden chains and a belt and breechcloth that barely covered her treasure. When she took off the bra and only a scrap of silk covered her, Doug Spencer's pants looked like they might split open.

Charlie wore a costume too, a harem guard, they said, and he looked good in what there was of it. He posed with her, his stomach and chest bare and hard with muscles. Mostly he posed behind her, but sometimes he stood over her while she sat at his feet. Every time he touched her, she thought she might come.

All the time, the other five men clicked intently, spellbound as she was, their cameras touching her, chasing the light along her curves, fondling her breasts and bringing the nipples to explosive, sensitive peaks, molding the tight curve of her thighs and hips. She turned before them, showing her bare bottom, aware that if she bent only a little, they would see the spread lips of her treasure.

But she kept that from them.

Then, late in the afternoon, the light beyond the windows ruby and gold, she wore the last costume, a tattered white shift that left her breasts and almost all of her legs bare. Charlie had stripped down to a single band of white cloth, the idea being that she and he were slaves together to a wicked sultan.

"Now, Desi," Mr. Bentley said, his voice warm and breathless. "Take off the dress."

She did not hesitate, her heart trilling with power and excitement, but she held them in the infinite compliance of her motion, not pulling it over her head but letting the thin straps fall from her shoulders and the fabric pool around her waist, standing to roll it over her hips and down.

With a little gesture of submissive flirtation, Desi stepped quickly out of the white cotton and dropped it, finally naked before them.

The light on her treasure thrilled her, their eyes, their desire, pulsed through her sex. She welcomed them, wanted them, soared into an ecstasy that their eyes would drink, their cameras record. Charlie's hands rested on her hips as ripples of pleasure flowed from her treasure, through her core, her heart, her fingers and toes, and she came right there, immortal on their film.

Scheherazade. That was who she was. The servant of these men and their mistress, and the thousand and one tales had only begun to be told.

"Oh, baby!" Bobby exclaimed to her in the car on the way home. "That was the best. You're incredible."

"I liked it," Desi laughed, drunk beyond the wine. "I liked it a lot."

Mr. Bentley, his gaze hot and flashing, had handed her a one hundred dollar tip. Dr. Barlow gave her fifty and the other men pooled another hundred. They wanted her to come back, but Desi didn't commit. Another idea bloomed in her soul.

"Bobby?" she asked. "You ever been to San Francisco?'

"Once," he said. "Why?"

"We could go out there," she said, resting her hand on his

thigh as the car rumbled down the lane leading away from Bentley's house. "I could be a model and you could be my photographer."

"That's..." he started to say and then he laughed. "Why not? You're amazing and you make me amazing. Those pictures I took the other day—they're the best I've taken—well, until today."

"Bobby," she said, her hand running up his thigh. "I watched you today. You weren't like the others." She stroked the line of his penis under his pants and he stirred, but only a little.

They rode in silence for a few minutes.

"Baby," he said. She heard the serious sound of his voice as he hunted for words. "When them other guys shoot you, they want to make love to you. When I do, it's 'cause I see how beautiful you are and I want to *be* you. You dig?"

Her gut tightened at the candid confession, but now, after this day, she understood and it was all right with her, maybe better than all right. Certain kinds of jealousy would never be an issue between them.

"Bobby, I've never felt so beautiful," she said, resting her head on his shoulder. "And I want to go to California with you."

Stu Gilbert turned the envelope in his hands, his brow furrowing at the postmark: Oakland, California. He tore the paper and smiled his naughty twelve-year-old smile.

Four months into 1959 and somebody had sent him a calendar worth hanging in his office. He leafed through it, regretting that he had missed January, February, and March, figuring he at least owed them a look.

When he flipped the page to April, he stopped breathing.

Desi! His Desi smiled back at him without a stitch on her, every bump on her pretty nipples sharp and clear as if painted with God's own hand. She winked at him. His smile split his face as he admired her mink bush and her legs spread just a little to show perfect pussy lips.

Stu's boner didn't go down till he made it to the john and jacked the toilet full of cream. He came back to his office and reverently, like a priest with a cross, hung the calendar over his desk, where it was a shrine for the rest of the month, to every one of the mechanics and the parts guys and half the customers. Stu grinned wickedly watching some of the women blush, but they couldn't take their eyes off her.

When the month ended, Stu very carefully tore the page from the calendar and put it with April, 1958, in a folder he had found between the ledgers.

He scratched his neck as he wandered toward the john, his cock rubbing against his trousers, the image of Desi's snatch vivid in his mind.

April, 1958 was pretty. April, 1959 was the sexiest thing he'd ever seen.

What the hell would 1960 bring?

ABOUT THE AUTHORS

CHEYENNE BLUE combines her two passions in life and writes travel guides and erotica. Her erotica has appeared in many anthologies, including *Best Women's Erotica, Mammoth Book of Best New Erotica, Best Lesbian Erotica, Best Lesbian Romance*, and on many websites. You can read more of her erotica at www.cheyenneblue.com.

Born in Virginia and later raised on a sailboat, **ANGELA CAPERTON** has traveled extensively and appreciates the world in all its forms. Her erotic fantasy, *Woman of the Mountain*, won the 2008 Eppie for Best Erotica, and she has short stories in *Lust at First Bite* and *Girls on Top*.

ELIZABETH COLDWELL is the editor of the U.K. edition of *Forum*. Her stories have appeared in anthologies including *Spanked: Red Cheeked Erotica; Yes, Sir* and *Best Women's Erotica 2009*. One of these days she'll get round to having a webcam installed.

ANDREA DALE's stories have appeared in *Do Not Disturb* and *Afternoon Delight,* among many others. With coauthors, she has written *A Little Night Music* and *Cat Scratch Fever.* "Now You See Her" is a companion story to "Come to My Window," in *Where the Girls Are.* More at www.cyvarwydd.com.

GENEVA KING (www.genevaking.com) has stories appearing in over a dozen anthologies including: *Ultimate Lesbian Erotica 2009, Ultimate Undies, Caramel Flava,* and *Travelrotica for Lesbians 1* & *2.* A transplant to Northern MD, she's constantly on the prowl for her next muse.

LOLITA LOPEZ started writing naughty tales to entertain friends as part of her coed procrastination. Study biochemistry or pen a quick story for her girlfriends? No surprise that she's on a sabbatical from college, eh? Lolita lives in Texas with her medic husband.

M. MARCH is the pseudonym of a writer who has contributed to the *New York Post,* AfterEllen, AfterElton, *Gay City News,* Blacktable.com, *Self, Complete Woman, Time Out New York, First-Timers* and *Spanked: Red-Cheeked Erotica.* Nonerotica interests include watching cult movies, browsing in bookstores, drinking strong coffee, and listening to obscure disco.

SOMMER MARSDEN bangs out her smut from a small cottage on the East Coast. She has appeared in dozens of print anthologies, numerous dirty magazines, and multiple filthy webzines. She is the author of multiple ebooks found at eXcessica, Whiskey Creek Press Torrid and Eternal Press. You can reach her at hot4sommer@yahoo.com.

L. A. MISTRAL has published five erotic novels with Renaissance ebooks and his short stories can also be seen in print in the Cleis publications *B Is for Bondage, Got a Minute?*, and *Hide and Seek*, and in *Bound to Love*. He also appears on the Ruthie's Club, Clean Sheets and Oysters and Chocolate websites.

NOBILIS REED takes care of his disabled wife, teenage kids, and too many cats, occasionally taking flights of erotic fancy that then become enmeshed in his brain until writing exorcises them. His career in smut has so far produced four novellas, which you can find at www.nobiliserotica.com.

JENNIFER PETERS is the associate editor of *Penthouse Forum* and *Girls of Penthouse* magazines. Her work has appeared in several places under numerous names, but her bylines in *Penthouse* and *Forum* are her favorites.

MALCOLM ROSS is the pseudonym of a happily married man (though not one with the same fetish as his protagonist) living deep in suburban Colorado. This is his first published story, though endless fantasies in his head are waiting to be written.

MONICA SHORES is a frequent contributor to *$pread* magazine, where she is also an editor. Her writing appears on Alternet, Boinkology, Popmatters, and filthygorgeousthings.com. While she does not particularly want to be pigeonholed as someone who writes only about sex, she's also not particularly interested in writing about anything else.

A country boy by breeding, **CRAIG J. SORENSEN** got his first Peep Show at an adult bookstore in New York City during a senior trip in high school. He's been peeping ever since, and parlays this fascination into his erotica. His work appears in anthologies and at various online locations including Clean Sheets.

SUSAN ST. AUBIN has been writing erotica for over twenty years. Her work has been published in *Yellow Silk, Libido, Herotica, Best American Erotica, Best Women's Erotica, Best Lesbian Erotica,* and many other journals and anthologies, as well as Cleansheets.com, Fishnetmag.com, and Forthegirls.com, and most recently in *Lust: Erotic Fantasies for Women.*

KISSA STARLING (www.kissastarling.com) is a woman of many words. Her stories range from sweet to sizzling and everything in between. What started as a few words written in a diary has turned into a full-fledged writing career. She spends time each and every day dreaming up plots, researching settings, and dreaming up characters.

DONNA GEORGE STOREY (www.donnageorgestorey.com) is the author of *Amorous Woman* (Neon/Orion). Her fiction has been published in numerous anthologies, including *Do Not Disturb: Hotel Sex Stories* and *X: The Erotic Treasury.* She writes a column, "Cooking up a Storey," for the Erotica Readers and Writers Association.

ABOUT THE EDITOR

RACHEL KRAMER BUSSEL (www.rachelkramerbussel.com) is an author, editor, blogger, and reading series host. She has edited or coedited over twenty books of erotica, including *Bottoms Up: Spanking Good Stories*; *Spanked*; *Naughty Spanking Stories from A to Z 1* and *2*; *The Mile High Club*; *Do Not Disturb*; *Tasting Him*; *Tasting Her*; *Yes, Sir*; *Yes, Ma'am*; *He's on Top*; *She's on Top*; *Caught Looking*; *Hide and Seek*; *Crossdressing*; *Rubber Sex*; *Sex and Candy*; *Ultimate Undies*; *Glamour Girls*; *Bedding Down*; and the nonfiction collections *Best Sex Writing 2008, 2009* and *2010*. Her work has been published in over one hundred anthologies, including *Best American Erotica 2004* and *2006*, Zane's *Chocolate Flava 2* and *Purple Panties, Everything You Know About Sex Is Wrong, Single State of the Union* and *Desire: Women Write About Wanting*. She serves as senior editor at *Penthouse Variations,* and wrote the popular "Lusty Lady" column for the *Village Voice.*

Rachel has written for *AVN, Bust,* Cleansheets.com, *Cosmopolitan, Curve,* Fresh Yarn, the Frisky, Gothamist, Huffington

Post, Mediabistro, *Newsday, New York Post, Penthouse, Play-girl, Radar, San Francisco Chronicle, Tango, Time Out New York*, and *Zink,* among others. She has appeared on "The Martha Stewart Show," "The Berman and Berman Show," NY1, and Showtime's "Family Business." She has hosted In The Flesh Erotic Reading Series since October 2005, which has featured everyone from Susie Bright to Zane, about which the *New York Times*'s UrbanEye newsletter said she "welcomes eroticism of all stripes, spots and textures." She blogs at lustylady.blogspot.com.

Check out the official *Peep Show* blog at peepshowbook. wordpress.com.